Thornton Wilder and Ken Ludwig's

adaptation of

THE BEAUX' STRATAGEM

by
George Farquhar

SAMUEL FRENCH

FOUNDED 1830

New York   Hollywood   London   Toronto

www.SAMUELFRENCH.com

ISBN 978 0 573 65053 6   **Printed in U.S.A.**   **#25634**

IMPORTANT BILLING AND CREDIT
REQUIREMENTS

Thornton Wilder and Ken Ludwig's
adaptation of
THE BEAUX' STRATAGEM
by George Farquhar

World Premiere Produced by
Shakespeare Theatre Company

Michael Kahn	Nicholas T. Goldborough
Artistic Director	Managing Director

This adaptation of *THE BEAUX' STRATAGEM* was first produced by the Shakespeare Theatre Company in Washington, D.C. (Artistic Director Michael Kahn, Managing Director Nicholas T. Goldsborough) from November 7 to December 31, 2006. The set was designed by James Kronzer, the Costume Designer was Robert Perdziola, the Lighting Designer was Joel Moritz, the Sound Designer was Martin Desjardins, the Choreographer was Peter Pucci, and the Fight Director was Paul Dennhardt. The production was under the direction of Michael Kahn with the following cast:

Boniface	DREW ESHELMAN
Cherry	COLLEEN DELANY
Daniel	MATTHEW STUCKY
A Lady	DIANE LIGON
Jack Archer	CHRISTOPHER INNVAR
Tom Aimwell	CHRISTIAN CONN
Gloss	RICK FOUCHEUX
Mrs. Kate Sullen	VEANNE COX
Dorinda	JULIA COFFEY
Lady Bountiful	NANCY ROBINETTE
Scrub	HUGH NEES
A Country Woman	ANNE STONE
Sullen	IAN BEDFORD
Servants	MARIA KELLY, DAVID MURGITTROYD
Hounslow	DAN CRANE
Bagshot	NICK VIENNA
Sir Charles Freeman	DANIEL HARRAY
Foigard	FLOYD KING

CAST

in order of appearance

BONIFACE, *landlord of an inn*
CHERRY, *the landlord's daughter*
DANIEL, *the landlord's servant*
A LADY, *set upon by robbers and disconcerted by it*
JACK ARCHER, *a gentleman of broken fortune, acting as a servant*
TOM AIMWELL, *a gentleman of broken fortune, acting as his master*
GLOSS, *a man of two professions, highwayman and clergyman*
MRS. KATE SULLEN, *Lady Bountiful's daughter-in-law*
DORINDA, *Lady Bountiful's daughter*
LADY BOUNTIFUL, *a country gentlewoman, foolishly fond of her son*
SCRUB, *servant to Sullen*
A COUNTRY WOMAN, *seeking medical advice*
SULLEN, *Lady Bountiful's son, brutal to his wife*
SERVANTS, *serving in the Sullen Household*
HOUNSLOW, *a highwayman*
BAGSHOT, *a highwayman*
SIR CHARLES FREEMAN, *Mrs. Sullen's brother*
FOIGARD, *a French parson anxious to perform a wedding*

SCENE OF THE ACTION

Lichfield, England, 1707

NOTES ON THIS ADAPTATION

For more than 200 years this celebrated late Restoration comedy, with its timelessly wicked and witty observations about society and differences between the sexes, was one of England's most popular and performed comedies. First produced in 1707, *The Beaux'*, as it is known familiarly, is still produced occasionally in England. But in this country, while routinely included in anthologies of Restoration drama, *The Beaux'* is rarely seen on stage outside a university or conservatory setting.

In the fall of 1939, with the goal of making it more accessible to a modern audience, Thornton Wilder began, but never completed, an adaptation of *The Beaux' Stratagem.* In 2004, Ken Ludwig accepted the invitation offered by the Wilder estate to finish the work. The completed play, sixty-seven years in the making, was produced with great success in 2006 by the Shakespeare Theatre Company in Washington, D.C.

THE MAKING OF THE WILDER-LUDWIG *BEAUX'*

Remarks by Tappan Wilder, Thornton Wilder's nephew and literary executor, and Ken Ludwig, to the cast and production company of *The Beaux' Stratagem* at the first rehearsal of the play, held on September 24, 2006.

Once upon a time, when I was reading Thornton Wilder's manuscripts in Yale's Beinecke Rare Book and Manuscript Library, where it's so quiet you are afraid to breathe, I came across the script of his unfinished adaptation of George Farquhar's celebrated *The Beaux' Stratagem*. It has been part of Wilder's archives for decades, but nobody appears to have paid any attention to it. As I read it, I started laughing so hard that a starchy scholar working at a nearby table gave me a public dressing down. That was my introduction to Thornton Wilder's take on *The Beaux' Stratagem.*

Where does this play fit into Wilder's career? My uncle entered the decade of the '30s, when he was in his 30s, determined to achieve Broadway standing. He had many an asset to help make this happen. He was a world-famous, Pulitzer-Prize winning novelist by this time, which meant that many doors were open to him. He had also been writing drama from boyhood on, and publishing plays from college on — and destroying them, too. By nature, Wilder wasn't a "keeper." Starting young, he threw away reams of material. ("I don't want future scholars to be bothered," he said later, adding his much-quoted line: "A wastepaper basket is a writer's best friend.") One of the plays he wrote as a young man was a Restoration comedy. It has not survived.

Another asset was his erudition, a talent on parade in his role as a celebrated teacher of classics in translation (part-time at the University of Chicago during the '30s), as well as his proficiency in French, German, Italian and Spanish that allowed him to read plays in their native tongue. It is no surprise, then, that he first got to Broadway by way of translation and adaptation. He translated André Obey's *Lucrece* from the French for Katharine Cornell in 1932. The play, which Cornell called her "favorite failure," died after only 31 performances. (Five years later, the admired British actor Brian Aherne, who played the villainous Tarquin in this show, was apparently slated for a major role in *The Beaux'*.)

Wilder's first Broadway success was another adaptation/translation, this time, in part, from German sources —a new stage version of *A Doll's House* for Jed Harris and Ruth Gordon. He finished this task in the spring of 1937 before departing for Europe to write plays buzzing in his own head. *A Doll's House* opened that summer in Central City, Colorado; played that fall with enormous success in the Midwest; and opened on Broadway at the end of 1937. The production set the record for the longest running *Doll's House* on Broadway —144 performances — a feat unsurpassed until 1997.

These adaptations and translations were followed by Wilder's innovative *Our Town*, which opened February 4, 1938, and which has never closed. He wound up 1938 with another adaptation, a freeranging adaptation, if you will, of a Johann Nestroy comedy he called *The Merchant of Yonkers*. It died a quick death, although everyone who mattered knew it would someday be a success. In the early 1950s Ruth Gordon picked it up and, with minor changes by Wilder, turned it in 1954 into *The Matchmaker*, the playwright's biggest success on Broadway.

By the end of the 1930s, an exhausted Wilder informed family and friends that he planned to devote the fall of 1939 to catching up on promised odd jobs, among them an introduction for an edition of Sophocles' *Oedipus Rex* (completed but not published until 1955) and an essay on playwriting (published in 1941 as "Some Thoughts on Playwrighting"). Then he consulted with Sol Lesser, the producer making a film of *Our Town*. Wilder had not counted on this diversion, which involved face-to-face meetings, telegrams, constant letters, etc., leaving him with little time to work on a project promised at the request of theatre producer Cheryl Crawford with, we believe, the added interest of the British-born actress/producer/director Margaret Webster — an adaptation of *The Beaux' Stratagem*. He started work on this task in September, just as war was declared in

Europe. By early December, he realized that he had lost his way with it and must give it up, although Crawford apparently had reserved a Broadway address for the show. In 1940, he began writing *The Skin of Our Teeth*, a new play of his own that spoke to the times.

Given his propensity for destroying paper, it speaks well for his view of its merits that Thornton Wilder preserved the record of his unfinished *Beaux'*. And I, for one, certainly never forgot my encounter with dramatic events in Lichfield. In fact, after that memorable day in the Beinecke, I began to dream of finding the right playwright to finish the play. Two years ago at the Alley Theater in Houston, Texas, I met Ken Ludwig. By chance we fell to talking about a subject of abiding interest to him, Restoration comedy. And here we are!

—Tappan Wilder

***

When Thornton Wilder began adapting *The Beaux' Stratagem* for a modern audience, he did something that few if any other playwrights have ever done before. Normally, when a dramatist chooses an underlying work to adapt, that work is in a different language, or it is in another medium altogether, be it a novel, a poem or, lately, a movie. What Wilder did was take a play written in English and create an adaptation of it in English, set in the same time period with almost all of the same characters. And the original work itself was already considered a minor classic of Restoration comedy.

As he sat with the original text in front of him, I imagine that Wilder must have been thinking something along the following lines: "Here is a great piece of theatre with remarkable comic exuberance, gloriously funny characters and an abundance of genuinely witty dialogue; and it sits on the shelf, unperformed for decades at a time, especially in this country, because it is too long; contains too many turgid, unedited passages, and features two minor characters who are given far too much stage time and whose 18th-century stereotypes (the funny Frenchman and the funny Irishman) leave us cold today. So why don't I pick this piece up and shake it a bit. I'll keep the exuberant storyline, the major characters and the great speeches. But I'll cut out all the boring bits, and, to make up for the cuts, add some new plot twists, some new characters and write some new scenes. Then, perhaps, I will be able to restore this play to the glory it deserves as a true classic of the 18th century, ready to stand beside its only peers, *She Stoops to Conquer, The Rivals* and *The School for Scandal.*"

Thornton Wilder was famously generous about acknowledging literary influences. His view of literature was that we are a part of a great continuum — a literary fellowship — and we stand upon the shoulders of the great writers who came before us. He once said, "Literature has always more closely resembled a torch race than a furious dispute among heirs." His work on the *Beaux'*, unfinished as it is, is a case study in the tradition he loved best. Here he was, some three hundred years along, standing on the shoulders of George Farquhar. And now I get to stand on the shoulders of both of these great writers. And so, in working on this play, when I got to a particular scene or speech that needed to be written anew or changed, I would ask myself two questions. First, what would Wilder or Farquhar do in this passage if he were standing in my shoes? And then – the ultimate question – what would the three of us do if we were working together right now, collaborating, and preparing for opening tonight?

— *Ken Ludwig*

A detailed review of the making of this adaptation will appear in the forthcoming collection of Thornton Wilder's translations and adaptations to be published by Theatre Communications Group Press (TCG). This volume, for which Ken Ludwig has contributed the Preface, will include both the completed adaptation of *The Beaux'* and Wilder's original fragment.

ACT I
Scene 1

(The hall of the inn, Saturday. ENTER BONIFACE from the yard.)

BONIFACE. *(Shouting)* Daniel! Cherry! Is everyone asleep? Are you all dead? Daniel! Daughter Cherry!

(ENTER DANIEL from the kitchen, and CHERRY on the balcony.)

CHERRY. Here! Here! Why do you bawl so?

BONIFACE. The company of the London coach has stood in the yard this hour and nobody to show them to their rooms. And, Daniel, there's a gentleman that has come by horse with his servant — help them in.

DANIEL. Yes, sir.

BONIFACE. And Cherry — hark'ee — there is a woman there, weeping and wailing that some highwaymen have robbed her. The London coach found her by the side of the road, half naked.

CHERRY. Poor woman!

BONIFACE. *(Whispering)* Faith, it was our highwaymen

that were on the road today; can there be any others that are serving this district?

CHERRY. Aye, there can. The work has become so easy and profitable that the highwaymen will soon be feeding on one another.

(The door is suddenly filled with an enormous woman, who staggers into the room. CHERRY runs and supports her.)

THE LADY. Thieves! Robbers! Where's the militia? God's oath, was ever woman so insulted!

CHERRY. Madam, calm yourself. You're safe here.

THE LADY. Devils and demons! The rogues rifled me and pulled me about like a rag doll! I'll send the militia after them or I am no true woman!

BONIFACE. Come, madam, your anger will do you more harm than the highwaymen, that's the truth. Cherry, help the lady up the stairs — gently! Gently!

THE LADY. (*On the stairs.*) Scurvy fellows, mousing and mussing me about and searching me under my clothes where they have no business. It's a miracle, sir, that I wasn't ravished! (*And she's gone.*)

BONIFACE. Faith, I'd have left her alone too...

(ARCHER ENTERS, followed by DANIEL, bowed down with boxes, bandboxes, etc.)

ARCHER. A room for my master, landlord, and dinner as soon as you're ready, for we've ridden many miles today. And make it the best you have.

BONIFACE. Aye, sir. The best it shall be. Daniel, carry

the luggage up to the Rose and Thistle, our best room, sir. Does your master stay long in town, one way and another?

(DANIEL goes upstairs with the luggage.)

ARCHER. I can't tell you, one way and another.

BONIFACE. Ah. And he is coming from…?

ARCHER. Where he began.

BONIFACE. And going to…?

ARCHER. Where he'll end up.

BONIFACE. I see. But can you tell me your master's name?

ARCHER. His name, sir? He's not come to you to be christened, sir. But here he is; if you want his name you can ask him yourself. *(ENTER AIMWELL.)*

BONIFACE. Welcome, sir, you're welcome. I'm old Will Boniface, pretty well known upon this road, one way and another.

AIMWELL. Mr. Boniface, your servant.

BONIFACE. And what will your honor please to drink?

AIMWELL. I have heard your town of Lichfield famed for its ale. I think I'll taste that.

(As BONIFACE draws the ale, AIMWELL turns on ARCHER.)

AIMWELL. Well, well, — gawking, staring, idling. Was ever man cursed with such a dolt? I wager this servant of mine has been telling you everything about me?

BONIFACE. Not a word, your worship.

AIMWELL. The dog blabs without prompting. God's faith, I wonder I have the patience to keep the fellow in my service. There's a fellow, landlord, if you bring him a dram or a coaxing wench, will tell everything he knows and a deal more. *(To ARCHER.)* Sirrah, don't forget to go to the stables and see my horses well-rubbed.

(ARCHER starts out the door.)

AIMWELL. No, no, first carry these to my room! One would think the fellow had never seen service before, though his father was hanged for miscounting spoons.

(ARCHER goes upstairs.)

AIMWELL. So you're proud of your ale, landlord?

BONIFACE. Aye, tis smooth as oil, sweet as milk, clear as amber, and strong as the odor of a good woman. Your health, sir.

AIMWELL. 'Tis confounded strong.

BONIFACE. It must be so, or how should we be strong that drink it? Ah, I remember the first glass of it was drunk by my Lady Bountiful, God bless her soul, when she'd come to see my daughter Cherry christened at the font.

AIMWELL. Lady Bountiful?

BONIFACE. Od's my life, sir, we'll drink her health. — My Lady Bountiful is one of the best of women. Her second husband left her worth a thousand pound a year and I believe she lays out half of it in charitable uses. She's very strong on doctoring, y' know, and cures almost as many as she kills.

AIMWELL. Doctoring?

BONIFACE. Aye, she treats rheumatisms, ruptures and wind in men; greensickness, obstructions and convulsions in

women. And I've noticed that once her patients visit her —
just the one time — they never go back again, that's how
good she is.

AIMWELL. Has this Lady Bountiful a family?

BONIFACE. She has a daughter that's called Dorinda —
the finest woman in all our country and the greatest fortune.
I drink her health.

AIMWELL. Handsome, and a fortune! Surely, she's
married.

BONIFACE. No, sir, though there's many as would like
to. Lady Bountiful has a son, too, Squire Sullen, we'll drink
his health!

AIMWELL. What sort of a man is he?

BONIFACE. Why, sir, the man's well enough. Says little, thinks less and does nothing at all. But he's a...he wants it
here, sir. (*Tapping his head.*)

(*CHERRY comes along the balcony.*)

BONIFACE. There's my daughter now. Cherry, is the
lady comfortable?

CHERRY. Aye, sir, she snores like a broken bagpipe.
Good day, sir.

BONIFACE. Daughter, I was just telling this gentleman,
— I don't know your name, sir?

AIMWELL. Why sir, I would not burden your memory
with it.

BONIFACE. No, sir. — I was telling him about Squire
Sullen.

CHERRY. He was here until three this morning and has
broken all the windows in the tap-room for the tenth time.

BONIFACE. 'Tis a fact, sir, he's never at home, though he married a fine lady from London four years back — Mrs. Sullen — we'll drink her health, sir.

CHERRY. Your servant, sir.

(CHERRY EXITS. ARCHER appears on the balcony.)

BONIFACE. Now what will your worship please to have for supper? The world resides under my roof, sir. Anything you please.

AIMWELL. Have you any veal?

BONIFACE. We're out of it.

AIMWELL. A nice trout?

BONIFACE. Sold the last of it this morning.

AIMWELL. Have you got any wildfowl?

BONIFACE. Um, no. We have a delicate pair of rabbits, sir.

AIMWELL. Fine.

BONIFACE. Fricasseed or smothered with onions.

AIMWELL. Smothered with onions.

BONIFACE. We're out of onions.

AIMWELL. Fricasseed then, and when you're ready.

BONIFACE. Yes, sir. (*EXIT*)

AIMWELL. So, Archer, welcome to Lichfield! Our adventure has begun! Tell me, Jack, how feels it to be a servant?

ARCHER. You gave me a deuced bad character just now. Just wait till Nottingham, when I shall be master and you servant. Then you'll hear things.

AIMWELL. Then at Lincoln you'll be under the stairs again.

ARCHER. And at Norwich, I'll mount 'em. — Nay, I like it. We're men of intrinsic merit, Tom, who can strike our fortunes out for ourselves. We have heads to get money and hearts to spend it.

AIMWELL. (*Touching the strong-box.*) But this last two hundred pounds —

ARCHER. Why let me tell you, those two hundred pound, with the experience that we are masters of, is a better estate than the two thousand we have spent. Now, I am for risking one of our hundred, if you will, upon this knight-errantry — to find one of us a rich wife and share the fortune down the middle, halves each — ; but in case we fail, we'll reserve the other hundred to carry us to some battlefield, where we may die, as we lived, in a blaze.

AIMWELL. With all my heart, and we have lived, — there's no doubting that, Jack. We won't say that we spent our fortunes, but that we enjoyed'em.

ARCHER. Right! So much pleasure for so much money. And had I millions, I would go to the same market again. Oh, London! London! Well, we have had our share and let us be thankful; past pleasures, for aught I know, are best; those to come may disappoint us. But hark'ee, Tom, I'll marry no *ugly* heiress however rich she be. I love hunting, but would not like Actaeon be eaten by my own dogs. Now tomorrow is Sunday. You can go to Church and scrape what acquaintance you can there, and I shall inquire in the kitchen as to what rich fortunes are settled hereabouts. But Tom, have you remarked the landlord's daughter; she has already given me a certain leer of invitation as the poet says.

AIMWELL. I confess I have not.

ARCHER. Good. 'Tis best so, for she is my adventure in

Lichfield, not yours. *(ENTER BONIFACE.)*

BONIFACE. The rabbits are on the fire, sir; you'll be served presently.

AIMWELL. Landlord, I have a small charge of money and your house is so full of strangers, that I believe it may be safer in your custody than in mine; for when this scurvy fellow of mine gets drunk he minds nothing. Just look at the dog, stooped over like a diseased rat. Here, Sirrah, reach me the strong-box.

ARCHER. Yes, your holiness.

AIMWELL. And take a bath for God's sake! He takes one once a year. They scrape him with a knife and he calls out "Lord Christ, I'm clean at last!" Here, landlord. The locks are sealed down, both for your security and mine, and it holds something above two hundred pound. Be sure you lay it where I may have it at a moment's warning. Perhaps I may be gone in half an hour; perhaps I may be your guest till the best part of that be spent; and pray order your ostler to keep my horses always saddled. Here, you dolt, show me to my room. And leave the servant girls alone this time!

(AIMWELL and ARCHER disappear into AIMWELL's room.)

BONIFACE. Cherry! Cherry!

(ENTER CHERRY with a tray from the kitchen.)

CHERRY. Yes, father?

BONIFACE. Consider well and tell me what you make of those two men up there?

CHERRY. I don't know, but I know one thing, sure: that servant is no servant.

BONIFACE. Then what is he, girl? What are they both?

CHERRY. I know not.

BONIFACE. What is it that says he may stay half an hour, or may remain till half two hundred pound are spent? What is it that asks that his horse be always saddled? Won't give his name and will say nothing of his business? And that leaves this box —

CHERRY. A highwayman, father!

BONIFACE. Ten to one, and this is some new-fetched booty of his. Now could we find him out, the money were ours.

CHERRY. He don't belong to our men.

BONIFACE. And since he don't belong to our fraternity we may betray him with a safe conscience. Look'ee, child, we must go cunningly to work; proofs we must have. The gentleman's servant loves drink, I'll ply him that way; and his master says he's easily coaxed by a wench, which shall be your opening, as the saying goes.

CHERRY. Father, would you have me give my secret for his?

BONIFACE. Consider, child, there's two hundred pound at stake. — Now mind your business. *(EXIT BONIFACE.)*

CHERRY. *(To the audience.)* What a rogue my father is! My father! I deny it. I have lived with myself long enough to know that I am no daughter of his. My mother was a good free-hearted generous woman; only I can't tell how far her good nature might have extended for the benefit of her children. This landlord of mine, for I think I can call him no more, would betray his guest and risk his daughter's honor, all for two hundred pounds. I wouldn't do it for five hundred. Or eight or nine. A thousand possibly, but that's real money.

And as for that fellow upstairs, I would rather he were a highwayman than a footman, for if he be a footman he has no future and is as misbegotten as I am.

(She goes up the stairs and knocks on AIMWELL'S door.)

CHERRY. Sir, your master's dinner's ready.

(ENTER ARCHER.)

ARCHER. Friend, your knock startled me. I was thinking of you at this very moment.

CHERRY. Of me, sir?

ARCHER. My master is so severe with me that I was afraid you would gather a low opinion of my merits.

CHERRY. Why, sir, my judgments are my own.

ARCHER. Good, for there is no one in Staffordshire by whom I would rather be well thought on.

CHERRY. Why sir, flattery is no way to bring it about.

ARCHER. Then let me wrestle for your good opinion. *(He does.)*

CHERRY. Sir! Tell yourself that I am the landlord's daughter in this inn; that there is no advance that you are likely to make which I have not fought off a hundred times, and with these reflections carry your master's dinner to him, for I think he is hungry.

(Starts to go. He tries to kiss her again but she pushes him away.)

ARCHER. I would fain make love to you, so render me the formula and tell me what to say.

CHERRY. Well then ask me a question about love and I'll answer it.

ARCHER. What is Love?

CHERRY. Love is I know not what, it comes I know not how, and goes I know not when.

ARCHER. Where does Love enter?

CHERRY. Into the eyes.

ARCHER. And where go out?

CHERRY. I won't tell you.

ARCHER. What are objects of that passion?

CHERRY. Youth, Beauty, and Clean Lips.

ARCHER. The reason?

CHERRY. The first two are fashionable in Nature; the third is a personal preference.

ARCHER. What are the signs and tokens of that passion?

CHERRY. A stealing look, a stammering tongue, words improbable, designs impossible, and actions impracticable. And since you are so bold as to furnish surmises about me, friend, I shall offer the same to you.

ARCHER. And what is that, my angel?

CHERRY. You are no footman, and why you are in this disguise, I think I know, too.

ARCHER. 'Sdeath! You are a witch in every way. Give me a kiss. (*He kisses her.*)

BONIFACE. (*Off*) Cherry! Cherry!

CHERRY. Mmmm — my father calls. You plaguey devil, how durst you stop my breath so? — Offer to follow me one step, if you dare!

(ARCHER EXITS into the room with his master's tray as BONIFACE ENTERS.)

BONIFACE. Well, daughter, have you smoked him out?

CHERRY. Pray, father, don't put me upon getting anything out of a man again. I'm but young and I don't understand wheedling.

BONIFACE. Don't understand wheedl —? You're a woman — it comes natural.

(ENTER from the yard MR. GLOSS.)

GLOSS. Landlord! Landlord!

BONIFACE. Oh, Mr. Gloss!

GLOSS. Is the coast clear?

BONIFACE. What's the news?

GLOSS. Four little encounters on the road — "stick 'em up," ha! ha! — all fair, square and honorable, that's all. Here, my dear Cherry, lay these with the rest. Nearly fifty sterling pounds. No one interfered with, and the transactions closed friend to friend!

BONIFACE Aye, I think we have one of your recent friends in the house: a large woman, she hath had the convulsions the greater part of this hour.

GLOSS. I remember her well. Wanted to be ravished. We had to keep denying her. Now let's see...Here are three wedding rings or — funeral rings — 'tis much the same, you know. Their owners begged me for them on their knees and, faith, I was moved to tears, though I do confess it. But I had almost forgot, my dear Cherry, I have a present for you.

CHERRY. What is it?

GLOSS. A pot of cerise, child, that I took out of the lady's underpocket.

CHERRY. What! Mr. Gloss, do you think I paint?

GLOSS. Why, your betters do. These things are but the usage of the world, my child, and when usage has made them acceptable, tis but cant and hypocrisy to cry out against 'em.

BONIFACE. Aye, Mr. Gloss. You reason wondrous clearly.

GLOSS. Thank you, sir. That comes from having a part-time occupation as chaplain of the militia. When I am not out on the road relieving women of their purses, I am a man of the cloth, restoring men to their souls. And do you know, I find that the sermons I preach in the camp are much benefited by my second profession on the road. When those I rob cry out *"Oh God! Oh God!"* I am reminded that He Above is the great giver of all that is good. And when, of a cold, damp night, they cry *"May you go to Hell!"* I am touched that they wish me the comfort of a warmer climate. And so, as the poet says, there be sermons in storms and good in everything.

BONIFACE. Do you know any other gentlemen of the pad that are now in the district?

GLOSS. No.

BONIFACE. I fancy that I have two that lodge in the house just now.

GLOSS. The devil!

BONIFACE. One of them pretends to be the servant of the other and is up in his master's room now serving him dinner. They have brought me a box to guard worth two hundred pound.

GLOSS. Doubtless some of these new fellows that cannot do the work of the road with honor and have brought the whole profession into bad repute.

BONIFACE. Look'ee, here comes the servant now, or the one that calls himself the servant.

(ENTER ARCHER above, cleaning boots.)

GLOSS. Mr. Landlord, draw us some ale and leave me alone with him. And you, Cherry, take my coat and secure these goods. Good evening, sir.

ARCHER. (*Descending*) Good evening.

GLOSS. Sir, the landlord has drawn some ale for us. Will you not have a glass with me? I am chaplain of the militia here. My name is Gloss.

ARCHER. Why, thank you, sir. I was on the way to the kitchen to ask this lady to join me in dinner.

BONIFACE. 'Twill be ready when you come. You'll have time for a talk with Mr. Gloss. Come, Cherry.

(EXIT BONIFACE and CHERRY.)

GLOSS. Your health, Mister …?

ARCHER. Uh, Martin. The name is Martin. (*They drink.*) There has been a hue and cry here for your militia, Mr. Gloss. There were highwaymen on the roads today. A poor woman was picked up by the London coach. She says she was nearly ravished.

GLOSS. Oh, I doubt that.

ARCHER. And that she was robbed, sir.

GLOSS. Of how much?

ARCHER. By her lamentations I should say it was a good deal.

GLOSS. Lamentations have nothing to do with it, Mr. Martin. I fancy some women make as much noise over the loss of a wedding ring as others make over two hundred pound.

ARCHER. Mr. Gloss, for a man of the cloth, you have a surprising clear insight into such matters.

GLOSS. And you, for a footman, Mr. Martin. I could swear on the Bible which I always have with me, — Devil take it, where's the plaguey thing gone — well, it's no matter, — I could swear on the Bible, sir, that you are no footman.

ARCHER. That's very strange, Mr. Gloss, because I could swear on the Bible, if you had one, that there's something in your face that is more than a chaplain. (*They both laugh.*)

GLOSS. Have I twigged you, Mr. Martin? Eh?

ARCHER. You are very sharp, sir.

GLOSS. Now, Mr. Martin, why should we not be above board with one another? You may be well-suited with your master as you call him; but I could do very well with a stout young fellow who's not afraid of a brisk moment or two on the road. However, we might begin lightly until we know one another better, so to speak. There's a piece of work in the neighborhood I have in mind. 'Tis in a house, sir, and the men I work with now are awkward boobies and would knock over every table in the way. They lack what I would call the light touch, as necessary in house-breaking as it is in religion.

ARCHER. You have henchmen, sir?

GLOSS. Aye, two fellows for the work on the road, and the innkeeper here and his daughter understand me, so to speak.

ARCHER. Mr. Boniface and his pretty daughter?

GLOSS. Aye, Cherry stores the goods and the landlord tells us the news of the road. Now, hark'ee, this house that I've mentioned will be easy pickings — with a deal of family plate that could be melted down, and I doubt not a good amount of money and jewels besides. Would such a venture interest you, Mr. Martin; you have only to think it over and give me a sign.

ARCHER. It shall have my full attention. You do me honor, Mr. Gloss.

GLOSS. Your servant, sir. *(GLOSS EXITS.)*

ARCHER. *(To the audience.)* Has one ever seen before such outright and arrant villainy? The man is a walking Babylon. I have been abroad, seen much and believed little. I have seen mountebanks disguised as doctors; speculators disguised as men of finance; and pick-pockets as attorney's at law; but never before have I met a highwayman disguised as a man of the cloth. Now there's a stratagem for you. Does not the poet say "Disguise, thou art a wickedness wherein the pregnant enemy does much?" Yet who am I to cast the first stone? Who does not wear the mask and apply the makeup? Look you, I am disguised as a footman at present, aimwell as a gentleman, Cherry as a maid. But Mr. Gloss, by *his* disguise and villainy means to violate some household and take their jewelry, plate and cash. Can I in good conscience stand by and watch such knavery, merely to preserve my own pretense? No — it cannot be. The world must be saved from its own inclinations; — and so my plan is this: I'll say yes to the villain and approve his script. But only until the eleventh hour, at which time, like young Prince Hal, "breaking through the foul and ugly mist of vapors," I'll expose his treachery, save the day, rescue the innocent and gain the undying love of the handsomest woman in all Staffordshire. Where is that woman, say you? Is it Cherry, the landlord's pliable daughter? No. Have we met her yet? No. But rest assured, she will turn up — for in a comedy, as opposed to life, the ending of the play is never in doubt. The only question is how we get there.

(He tips his hat, as it were, and EXITS.)

Scene 2

(LADY BOUNTIFUL'S house, Sunday morning. MRS. SULLEN and DORINDA are stretched out in attitudes of complete boredom. ENTER LADY BOUNTIFUL followed by SCRUB carrying two large trays of medicaments.)

LADY BOUNTIFUL. Scrub, Scrub, are there many patients waiting for me this morning?

SCRUB. Yes, Milady, — There are two jaundices and a phlebotomy to my certain knowledge, —

LADY BOUNTIFUL. Indeed! Did you hear that my dears? It is not every morning that we have a phlebotomy, Scrub.

SCRUB. No, Milady, your phlebotomies are become monstrous rare. And Goodman Hodge is here again —

LADY BOUNTIFUL. Ah, that will be a pepper poultice, I think. Daughter-in-law Sullen, you must come and see me make a poultice, it is the most diverting sight in the world.

MRS. SULLEN. To tell the truth, Madam, I could not rise from this chair to see an amputation, for all the pleasure in't, could you, sister?

DORINDA. These Sunday delights are become so frequent here that the edge of pleasure is somewhat dulled.

LADY BOUNTIFUL. Is everything ready, Scrub? You

have not forgot anything? The vinegar? The flour? The bone saw?

MRS. SULLEN. Do not your patients object a little to the sawing of their bones?

LADY BOUNTIFUL. Oh, I only use it in extreme cases. Gangrene. Leprosy. Severe headache. Scrub, you have not one-fourth the hydrophil and binding we will use. And don't we have a delivery today? Where is that new head clamp? I'm most anxious to try it.

MRS. SULLEN. *(Aside to DORINDA.)* It makes one rather glad to have been born already.

LADY BOUNTIFUL. Remember, ladies, men with fortunes may come and go, but a good head clamp lasts a lifetime. You are quite well, daughter-in-law? You look a little drawn.

MRS. SULLEN. I am in excellent health, Madam, to no purpose.

LADY BOUNTIFUL. You must keep up your strength, you know. My son, your husband, requires constant attention. He's of a sickly nature, more so even than most husbands.

MRS. SULLEN. He is drunk, madam; or was so when last I saw him.

LADY BOUNTIFUL. You are severe, daughter Sullen. He drinks entirely for his health. He has a poor constitution and finds that spirits restore his blood.

MRS. SULLEN. In that case, he must be the healthiest man in England.

LADY BOUNTIFUL. He will be up before long and will amuse you till church-time.

MRS. SULLEN. And to the same degree.

LADY BOUNTIFUL. Come, Scrub, we must to work. Two jaundices, you say?

SCRUB. Yes, milady, 'twill e'en do your heart good to see them. They are as yellow as oranges.

(Exeunt LADY BOUNTIFUL and SCRUB.)

DORINDA. You are for church this morning, sister-in-law?

MRS. SULLEN. Anywhere to pray, for Heaven alone can help me. But I think, Dorinda, there is no form of prayer in the liturgy against bad husbands.

DORINDA. But there's a form of law in the courts, and I swear that rather than see you thus, continually discontented, I would advise you to apply for that.

MRS. SULLEN. Heigh-ho!

DORINDA. And yet supposing, Madam, that you did bring it to a case of separation, what can you urge against your husband? My brother is, first, the most constant man alive. He never sleeps away from you.

MRS. SULLEN. *(Ruefully)* No, he is always there.

DORINDA. He allows you a maintenance suitable to your quality.

MRS. SULLEN. A maintenance! Do you take me, Madam, for a country orphan that I must sit down and bless my benefactors for meat and drink? I brought your brother a dowry of ten thousand pounds out of which I might expect a few pleasures.

DORINDA. You share in all the pleasures that the country affords.

MRS. SULLEN. Country pleasures! Racks and torments! I was not trained, child, in leaping of ditches and clambering over stiles — drinking fat ale, playing at whisk and making poultices with that good old gentlewoman my mother-in-law! But look, here is something come to divert us —

(ENTER a COUNTRYWOMAN.)

COUNTRYWOMAN. I come, an't please your Ladyship, — you're my lady Bountiful, an't ye?

MRS. SULLEN. Well, good woman, go on.

COUNTRYWOMAN. I come seventeen long mile to have a cure for my husband's sore leg.

MRS. SULLEN. Your husband! What, woman, cure a husband!

COUNTRYWOMAN. Aye, poor man, for his leg won't let him stir from home.

MRS. SULLEN. And what's the matter with his leg, Goody?

COUNTRYWOMAN. It come first, as one might say, with a sort of dizziness in his foot.

MRS. SULLEN. Aye, dizziness is very common in husbands.

COUNTRYWOMAN. Then he had a kind of laziness in his joints, and then his leg broke out, and then it swelled, and then it closed again, and then it broke out again, and then it festered, and then it grew better, and then it grew worse again.

MRS. SULLEN. Well, my good woman, I'll tell you what you must do. You must lay your husband's leg upon a table, and with a chopping knife you must lay it open as broad as you can.

COUNTRYWOMAN. Yes, your ladyship.

MRS. SULLEN. Then you must take out the bone, and beat the flesh soundly with a rolling pin; then take some salt, pepper and cloves and season it well. Then roll it up like brawn and put it in the oven for two hours.

COUNTRYWOMAN. Heaven reward your ladyship. I have two little babies, too, that are piteous bad with the gripes, an't please you.

MRS. SULLEN. Ah, that I know nothing about. My knowledge extends only to husbands, Goody, and is boundless.

(ENTER LADY BOUNTIFUL.)

LADY BOUNTIFUL. Daughters, daughter, you must come quickly, I am making ointment for the treatment of goiters and you don't want to miss it. I used it last week on one poor gentleman and his goiter has simply *doubled* in size! It looks like a cannon ball. Which is a good development, of course, because any time now, with the application of just a bit more ointment, it will explode and disappear. What's this, my good woman, have you come to see me?

MRS. SULLEN. I beg your ladyship's pardon for taking your business out of your hands. I have been atampering here with one of your patients.

LADY BOUNTIFUL. Come, good woman, don't mind this mad creature. I am the person that you want. The great healer. Now what is the problem?

COUNTRYWOMAN. Me husband's leg, ma'am. It's swole up like a sausage, fit to burst.

LADY BOUNTIFUL. A swollen leg. That will require the raccoon milk. He must bathe it in that twice a week. Come, it's in my dispensary — or at least a portion of it. As you can imagine, it is hard to gather in sufficient quantities, raccoons having such small breasts.

(COUNTRYWOMAN EXITS.)

LADY BOUNTIFUL. Daughter Sullen, how can you be merry with the misfortunes of other people?

MRS. SULLEN. Because my own make me sad, madam.

LADY BOUNTIFUL. Do not forget, pray, that I brought your husband back from death's door. We doubted of his life.

MRS. SULLEN. I was not here at the time, madam — I do not know how I could have bourn the suspense.

(EXIT LADY BOUNTIFUL.)

MRS. SULLEN. O, sister, sister! If ever you marry, beware of a sullen, silent sot, one that's always musing but never speaks. Think now: He came home this morning at his usual hour of four and wakened me out of a sweet sleep by tumbling over the tea table which he broke all to pieces; after his man and he had rolled about the room, like sick passengers in a storm, he comes flounce into bed, dead as a salmon into a fishmonger's basket; his feet cold as ice, his breath hot as furnace, and his face as greasy as a raw pork chop. O matrimony. He tosses up the clothes, disorders the whole economy of my bed, leaves me half-naked, and my whole night's comfort is the tuneable serenade of that wakeful nightingale his nose. But here he comes, and you shall see how handsomely he will beg my pardon.

(ENTER SULLEN. Stands silent. Then belches loudly.)

SULLEN. My head aches consumedly.

MRS. SULLEN. Will you be pleased, husband dear, to drink tea with us this morning? It will do your head good.

SULLEN. Tea gives me the wind. Scrub! Scrub!

(ENTER SCRUB.)

SCRUB. Sir!

SULLEN. What day of the week is't?

SCRUB. Sunday, an't please your worship.

SULLEN. Sunday? 'Twas Sunday t'other day!

MRS. SULLEN. Aye, every seventh, my love. You'll get the hang of it in time.

SULLEN. Bring me a dram. And set out the venison-pasty and a tankard of strong beer. I'll go to breakfast.

(Another loud belch and he's gone, followed by SCRUB.)

MRS. SULLEN. Inveterate stupidity! Did you ever know such a lump as this?! Nay, I shall never have good of the beast till I get him to town — Oh London, London is the place for managing a husband. A man dare not play the tyrant in London. Like all capitol cities, it is full of loose behavior. Wives get away with anything there.

DORINDA. Tell me, sister Sullen, if you are not angry with me for asking, why did you ever marry my brother?

MRS. SULLEN. He said beautiful things to me. Believe it or not. When a man is courting, he is not himself. He is the oil painting on which the sketch is based. Also, at that time I was on the point of making a no less grievous mistake, for I almost married a certain Lord Robert Aimwell, who has under marriage turned out to be a monster of avarice and cruelty, so report says.

DORINDA. In one way or another the story of all wives; and as for me I shall expect of no man anything more than

false appearance and deception, and am sure of nothing save
that I shall remain single to the end of time.

MRS. SULLEN. Now you are too earnest in this, and
henceforth I swear to speak only well of the marriage state;
for you should know the misfortune of my own has made me
all the more resolved that you shall be happily married.

DORINDA. Your labor, I fear, will be in vain.

MRS. SULLEN. Come, it is time to prepare for church,
— no, Dorinda, we shall find for you a husband with no
deception in him.

(A servant ENTERS.)

DORINDA. A husband and no deception. Is that an oxy-
moron?

MRS. SULLEN. Ox and moron describe many a husband, but this one shall be honest at least.

DORINDA. A bargain! *They go out.*

Scene 3

(ENTER MRS. SULLEN and DORINDA.)

MRS. SULLEN. Ha! ha! ha! my dear sister, let me
embrace thee! Now we are friends indeed; for I shall have a
secret of yours as a pledge for mine. I shall have you con-
versable in the subject of sex.

DORINDA. But do you think that I am so weak as to fall
in love with a fellow at first sight?

MRS. SULLEN. Pshaw! Now you spoil all; why should

not we be as free in our friendships as the men? I warrant you, the gentleman you saw just now in church has got to his confidant already, has avowed his passion, toasted your health, called you ten thousand angels, has run over your lips, eyes, neck, shape, air, and everything, in a description that warms their mirth to a second enjoyment.

DORINDA. Your hand, sister, I an't well.

MRS. SULLEN. So — she's breeding already. — Come, child, now tell me, don't you like the gentleman?

DORINDA. The man's well enough.

MRS. SULLEN. Well enough! Is he not a demigod, a Narcissus, a star, the man in the moon? Penelope herself, I warrant, waited in Ithaca for just such a man. O, here comes our Mercury!

(ENTER SCRUB.)

MRS. SULLEN. Well, Scrub, what news of the gentleman?

SCRUB. Madam, I have brought you a packet of news.

MRS. SULLEN. Open it quickly, come.

SCRUB. In the first place I inquired who the gentleman was; they told me, he was a stranger. Secondly, I asked what the gentleman was; they answered and said, that they never saw him before. Thirdly, I inquired what countryman he was; they replied, 'twas more than they knew. Fourthly, I demanded whence he came; their answer was, they could not tell. And, fifthly, I asked whither he went, and they replied, they knew nothing of the matter — and this is all I could learn.

MRS. SULLEN. But what do the people say? Can't they guess?

SCRUB. Why, some think he's a spy, some guess he's a mountebank; some say one thing, some another; and yet everyone admires his beauty.

MRS. SULLEN. Scrub. Listen. You must go right now and get acquainted with his footman. Invite him hither for a glass of ale.

DORINDA. What?

SCRUB. Yes, madam.

MRS. SULLEN. O, 'tis the best plot in the world! As you drink with him, *we* will drop in by accident and ask the fellow some questions.

(A servant ENTERS.)

SERVANT. Madam, dinner's upon the table.

MRS. SULLEN. Scrub, we'll excuse your waiting. I am Oberon, you are Puck. Go. Go! Look how you go, Swifter than arrow from the Tartar's bow!

SCRUB. Madam, I shall! *(SCRUB runs out.)*

Scene 4

(The Inn, Sunday after church. ENTER GLOSS, mopping his brow, followed by BONIFACE.)

BONIFACE. Come, Mr. Gloss, you will need a Sunday glass of ale, for I doubt not you preached a loud sermon and thumped the Bible soundly.

GLOSS. Faith, I was strong today, monstrous strong. The men wept like babies, Mr. Boniface, and a round dozen of them swooned away. I gave 'em the Judgment Day, sir. The

Judgment Day! And when I parted the sheep from the goats — did you not hear a kind of noise on the air?

BONIFACE. 'Tis true, sir. The camp is two miles away, but I heard a noise this morning like distant thunder.

GLOSS. Aye, that was the goats going to eternal damnation. When I think of sinners, Mr. Boniface, I cannot contain myself, I must let go.

BONIFACE. Sure, there's advancement for you in the church, Mr. Gloss. Have you thought of that?

GLOSS. You have hit upon it, sir! My fondest wish! Some day I hope to establish myself and make a name to be reckoned with. Which leads me to the matter at hand, sir, for I have come to ask you for the hand of your daughter Cherry.

BONIFACE. In marriage, Mr. Gloss? Why, this is a great honor, sir. Cherry is but young yet, but she's of an age to make up her own mind in these matters. I'll call her. Cherry! Cherry!

GLOSS. There's no time to be lost. I think I have noticed a certain understanding between your daughter and that young footpad upstairs.

BONIFACE. Cherry!

(ENTER CHERRY.)

CHERRY. Yes, Father?

BONIFACE. Daughter Cherry, our friend Mr. Gloss has something to say. to you. I'll leave you now.

(EXIT BONIFACE.)

GLOSS. My dear Cherry, all-wise providence has ordained the institution of marriage for the propagation of the race and the comfort of man. But it should not be entered into hastily. My dear Cherry, we have known one another for four years.

CHERRY. Yes, Mr. Gloss, since the day you were first arrested, started to cry and I loaned you me hanky.

GLOSS. Yes, yes. But, I've not failed to bring you presents, have I?

CHERRY. Thank you, sir. The first was the watch you stole from the Bishop.

GLOSS. That's not the point! Now, Cherry, I think I can say that I am held to be a man of substance —

CHERRY. Oh, yes. There's two hundred pounds on your head right now.

GLOSS. Why, Cherry, your thoughts run only on the business of the road; I am a man of the cloth, too, you know.

CHERRY. Mr. Gloss, if your addresses are directed to me, I thank you most humbly for the honor you do; but you may spare your pains, sir, for I have the unfortunate inclination, common to young women, of wishing to marry someone more nearly my own age. Or at least within twenty or thirty years.

GLOSS. Twenty or th — Aye, harkie, I know your drift. Your fancy's running on the footman that's upstairs. Well, there's your own age, minx, and a highwayman to boot.

CHERRY. 'Tis not certain, sir.

GLOSS. Not certain? Zounds! 'Tis as certain as sunrise, madam. For your Mr. Martin is about to engage with me this very night to enter Lady Bountiful's house and rob it, minx.

CHERRY. Lady Bountiful's? Mr. Gloss I'll not have it! Besides she is my godmother, she has done me and all my family a thousand kindnesses. Nay, I'll prevent it.

GLOSS. How, madam? Do you not know that any disclosure of this will bring you under the law also?

CHERRY. Mr. Gloss, I'll have no more to do with you. You shall have your presents back tonight, and I'll be no more the keeper of your stolen goods, sir, and you'll not take Mr. Martin with you in the shadow of the hangman's rope. If Mr. Martin be a highwayman, he is but new at it, and you'll not give him lessons.

(ARCHER ENTERS on the balcony.)

ARCHER. Good morrow, Mr. Gloss. Good morrow, Cherry.

CHERRY. Your servant, sir.

(CHERRY turns and goes out angrily.)

ARCHER. Is Cherry angry?

GLOSS. Is she a woman? Women are always angry. It's how they get things. Now Mr. Martin, have you considered the venture I spoke of?

ARCHER. Why, I'm warming to it, Mr. Gloss. Men of adventure can always use an extra coin or two. When is't to be?

GLOSS. I'm for it tonight, whether you decide to be of the party or no. Without you I'll take a likely assistant, but I'd prefer your company.

AIMWELL. (*From outside.*) Where's my servant? My servant, I say!

ARCHER. Wait — here comes my master. Would you have him in the business, too?

GLOSS. There's no need of him, Mr. Martin. The fewer the partners, the larger the portions, if you get my drift. And so, may I have your answer?

ARCHER. ...You may cut me in.

GLOSS. Excellent! Excellent! Your servant, sir.

(GLOSS EXITS into kitchen. ENTER AIMWELL from church in high spirits.)

AIMWELL. Jack! Our journey's over. Our results are assured, and there's nothing left to do but rejoice!

ARCHER. What, are you married already?

AIMWELL. No; but I marry this girl I saw at church or die a bachelor. Jack, such beauty, such eyes, such an air.

ARCHER. Is she rich, too?

AIMWELL. She is, Jack. I tipped the sexton of the church a shilling and have learned the necessaries. She has twenty thousand pound and a thousand a year, or thereabouts — but, faith, Jack, I know not how far I'd go had she nothing.

ARCHER. Fortunately, that's not in question. What's her name?

AIMWELL. Dorinda, which means golden, don't it, Jack, for you're a scholar.

ARCHER. Why, yes, there appears to be some gold in Dorinda.

AIMWELL. And she's the daughter of a good woman named Lady Bountiful that lives hard by.

ARCHER. What? Lady Bountiful? Why, I've been invited this morning to the very house. Their servant Scrub came here and asked me to drink with him. An excuse, surely, to allow the lady time to pump me of your name and quality. What name shall I give you, Tom?

AIMWELL. Why, I'll use my brother's since I'm not like to have anything else from the miser; and his title will aid the early steps of the business. I'll be Lord Robert Aimwell, 'twill fetch me to their house the sooner.

ARCHER. Mark you, your Lordship, how circumstance is playing into our hands.

AIMWELL. It is indeed. But we must devise a means whereby I, too, may enter the house, and as soon as possible, for every hour's separation from Dorinda is — but here is your friend; I'll leave you.

(ENTER CHERRY. AIMWELL goes up to his room.)

ARCHER. Good morrow, dear Cherry.

CHERRY. Your servant, Mr. Martin.

ARCHER. Mr. Martin! Did you not agree last night to call me Jack, and to kiss me for forfeit if you forgot it?

CHERRY. Mr. Martin, I am not the same woman you talked with last night; and I despise the ignorant, deluded foolish Cherry who stood right here twelve hours ago.

ARCHER. What? What's this? Wherein lies the difference?

CHERRY. Why, sir, I am wiser now. Now I know that the world is a wicked place; that ingratitude is the law of its being; and that men are deceivers all, all. Sir, can you tell the truth?

ARCHER. Yes.

CHERRY. Then will you answer three questions I put you?

ARCHER. If I may put three questions to you and be truly answered.

CHERRY. Agreed! Is your name Martin?

ARCHER. No!

CHERRY. Are you the servant you pretend to be?

ARCHER. No!

CHERRY. Did you tell Mr. Gloss that you would rob a house tonight?

ARCHER. Why, I —

CHERRY. Yes, or no?

ARCHER. Yes!

CHERRY. I am your servant, Mr. Martin.

ARCHER. My questions now! Do you shirk the contract, witch?

CHERRY. Put them!

ARCHER. Were you set on by someone else to wheedle information from me?

CHERRY. Yes.

ARCHER. Have you been the custodian of the goods that Mr. Gloss has stolen upon the road? Yes or no!

CHERRY. (*Bursting into tears.*) Yes.

ARCHER. Do you understand that circumstance can often force one into situations, my dear Cherry, where the appearance of evil is worse than the substance?

CHERRY. Oh, yes, Mr. Martin.

ARCHER. Then will you think well of me until such time as you will discover the worst?

CHERRY. (*Drying her eyes.*) Yes, I will.

ARCHER. Good. Cherry, listen to me. Your father is a rogue.

CHERRY. I know it.

ARCHER. Now within a few hours, Mr. Gloss will be apprehended, and I do not doubt that before the Justice he will reveal all the share which you and your father have had in his robberies. Let me advise you to take this store of money and hie yourself over to Ireland. Go tonight, Cherry, or it may be too late.

CHERRY. And will I never see you again, Mr. Martin?

ARCHER. Why when the hue and cry has died down, Cherry, you would best return to London; and inquire in the clubs for Jack Archer. Now, goodbye, pretty Cherry, and God speed!

CHERRY. God Bless, good sir!

(CHERRY kisses ARCHER fiercely and dashes from the room.)

ARCHER. *(To the audience.)* Good God, what a wench! A fine soul with rare eyes, a magnificent figure and easy virtue. Could any man ask for more that that? Of course she is a serving girl; but am I so lauded by society that I cannot think beyond the commonplace of expectation? Am I such a Presbyterian? Now I'll admit that she is helping a highwayman store his goods and could be sent to the gallows for her knavery at any moment. But if she were found to be with child, she would not be hanged as a matter of law. So perhaps, out of sheer goodness I should...no. I'll do my best to save this wench and look elsewhere for happiness. The philosophers say that happiness is found within. Whether or not I can find it in there myself is a mystery at the moment, but if I were you I wouldn't leave your seats.

(He EXITS quickly into his room.)

Scene 5

(LADY BOUNTIFUL's house, Sunday night. MRS. SULLEN
listening at a door from behind which come sounds of
men singing. ENTER DORINDA.)

DORINDA. What do you there, sister? What can it be?
Sure, there are a dozen men singing?

MRS. SULLEN. Three. My husband; Scrub; and a guest.

DORINDA. What guest is that?

MRS. SULLEN. You must think for yourself who it is.
— Lud, my husband can sing only one note.

DORINDA. Is it...is it Mr. Boniface?

MRS. SULLEN. No, child, no. I would not listen at a
door to hear Mr. Boniface singing. You must guess again.

DORINDA. Is it...? (*Suddenly*) Sister! Well, I'll not stay;
I'll not see him. Do you think that I am a fool to fall in love
with the first strange man that appears in church? No doubt
you have devised some way to bring him into the house, but
I'll not see him. Good day, madam.

MRS. SULLEN. (*Laughing*) Dorinda! Wait, sister. The
guest that you hear singing is not the gentleman you saw in
church; it is only his footman.

DORINDA. His footman!

MRS. SULLEN. You remember that I had Scrub ask him
to the house. They have fallen to drinking, and my husband,
who can scent where drinking is at twenty miles distance, has
joined them.

SULLEN. (*From offstage.*) Brother Martin! Into the
drawing room, we'll find the women.

MRS. SULLEN. Sh! They are coming. We will go into the china closet and overhear them.

DORINDA. Should we be eaves-droppers, sister?

MRS. SULLEN. Since they are drunk, their minds are absent, and it is no indiscretion to overhear a vacancy, I suppose. Come.

(Exeunt the ladies. ENTER SULLEN, SCRUB and ARCHER.)

SULLEN. Come, come brother Martin! The women are not here, and if they were 'tis no matter; for I'm master here and can break all the chairs and tables, too.

SCRUB. Your Worship! Your Worship! Remember your promise. You promised her ladyship on the bible and the stud-book that you'd break no more furniture. Recollect, your worship, — all the women weeping and all the glass in the dogs' feet.

SULLEN. Aye, aye, but Brother Martin, — harkee! — breaking a chair in a window is the greatest sport in the world. And I can afford it, too. Now you must call me Brother Sullen, for I'll drink and break chairs with no man but a brother. Why, brother Martin, you're as good a man as I am any day. Had your father married my mother, would y'not have owned this place, and married my wife, and no man would have known the difference? Come! Liquor came into this world to prevent thinking, so let's drink!

ARCHER. *(To SCRUB.)* Your master is more at home in his stable, I should say.

SCRUB. Aye, then he gets the dogs and horses drunk along with him.

SULLEN. 'Sdeath, I know not where the women are.

They were here an hour ago. 'Tis no matter, save only — hm!
— you must kiss my wife.

ARCHER. Eh?

SULLEN. She's a fine London lady and says we have no
pleasures in the country. You may kiss my sister, too, if you
will, but she's skim-milk. — Mrs. Sullen! Mrs. Sullen!

(EXIT SULLEN.)

ARCHER. Is she handsome, brother Scrub?

SCRUB. Extremely, sir. Though, as for myself, I've been
married twenty years and at this point a moose with the rick-
ets would look good to me.

(SULLEN ENTERS.)

SULLEN. Well, let her seek her own pleasures; I've
done my duty. — But tell me brother Martin, why have you
come into the country?

ARCHER. Hm! Can you keep a secret, brother Scrub?

SCRUB. I? I? I call his worship to witness. Have I not
kept all your worship's secrets? How you broke the china
shepherd that your wife got from London —

SULLEN. Hush! Hush!

SCRUB. And how your worship lost in the mud the letters that your wife gave you to post —

SULLEN. Sh! Devil take you!

SCRUB. Sure, I can keep a secret! — And how you
stood on her pet dog so that it sickened and had to be shot.

SULLEN. Hold your tongue! Death and damnation!

ARCHER. My secret is this: My master fought a duel t' other

day in London and wounded his man so dangerously that he thinks fit to withdraw till he hears whether the gentleman's wounds be mortal or not.

SULLEN. ...Nay, you shall kiss my wife! — Kate! Kate! — I shall find her for you. (*EXIT SULLEN.*)

ARCHER. Your master's wife must be unusually forgiving. Is he fond of her?

SCRUB. I believe he'd like her better if she were pickled in whiskey.

(ENTER MRS. SULLEN and DORINDA.)

MRS. SULLEN. Oh! You are not alone, Scrub?

SCRUB. No, Madam, this is Mr. Martin, the servant of the strange gentleman you saw in church today.

(MRS. SULLEN and ARCHER look at each other — and their mutual attraction at such close quarters is instant, strong and palpable — as though a piano wire were suddenly stretched taut between 'em.)

MRS. SULLEN. Mr. ...Martin?

ARCHER. Aye, madam...your humble servant.

MRS. SULLEN. A footman, sir?

ARCHER. Aye, madam.

MRS. SULLEN. How long have you served your present master?

ARCHER. Not long, madam. My life has been mainly spent in the service of the ladies.

MRS. SULLEN. And which service do you like best?

ARCHER. Oh the ladies, by a great deal.

MRS. SULLEN. Why is that?

ARCHER. (*Making love with his voice.*) Since your ladyship has asked...I may say there is a charm in their looks ...if they be handsome...that turns duty to inclination, and obligation to pleasure; to be near them is to feel a constant intoxication which removes fatigue; and to gaze upon them is a happiness which all but makes us forget the livery we wear.

MRS. SULLEN. Sir, if your present master is married, I presume you still serve a lady?

ARCHER. No, madam, I take care never to come into a married family. The commands of the master and mistress are so contrary that 'tis impossible to please both.

MRS. SULLEN. Come, I do not like my sister to hear marriage ill-spoken of, for I am resolved that she shall be happy in it.

ARCHER. Indeed, the young lady's chance of happiness in it will be the greater if her anticipations are not raised to too high a pitch. I am half persuaded that my master, should he chance to fall in love, would make the husband that the human race has waited for.

MRS. SULLEN. Sure, you are married yourself, sir?

ARCHER. No, madam, — unfortunately. The same livery which brings me into the service of ladies of quality has unfitted me for the society of women in my own station. The kindness of your question has brought to light the unhappiness of my life. For when I have the privilege of talking to a woman of quality, of beauty, madam, of elegance and wit, madam, — of admiring her fine eyes, — can you not conceive that I might forget that I am a servant and remember only that I am a man?

MRS. SULLEN (*Deeply affected by such lovemaking,*

out.) The devil take him for wearing that livery! Is it not a mischievous provoking world where such an address and such presence must be lowly footman!...(*To* DORINDA.) Come, sister, we must not detain them from their amusement. Sir, I thank you for this company. (*Giving* ARCHER *some money.*) Something for a pair of gloves.

ARCHER. I humbly beg leave to be excused. My master, Lord Robert Aimwell pays me, —

MRS. SULLEN. Lord Robert — ...?

ARCHER. (*Continuing*) — nor dare I take money from any other hands without injuring his honor and disobeying his command. Good day, Madam, — Madam. — Come, brother Scrub.

(Exeunt ARCHER and SCRUB.)

DORINDA. He said his master was Lord Robert Aimwell. Is not that the cruel and miserly gentleman you said was suitor to your hand in London? And is he not married now? And why did you not recognize him in church today?

MRS. SULLEN. Why, you're right! The man's an imposter, which means they both are. So this footman may not be a footman at all.

DORINDA. Hsst! My mother approaches.

(ENTER LADY BOUNTIFUL.)

LADY BOUNTIFUL. Did I not hear men's voices singing?

MRS. SULLEN. Yes, your ladyship. A London servant from the inn has been passing the hour with Scrub, and your son has joined them in their drinking. Purely for medicinal purposes, I'm sure.

LADY BOUNTIFUL. You make fun, daughter Sullen, but singing and drinking go well together, and singing is good medicine. It eases the doldrums and has a healing power. I sometimes sing to my patients and it works such wonders that they beg me to stop after just a few notes.

(ENTER ARCHER in haste.)

ARCHER. Saving your presence...where...where is Lady Bountiful? Pray which is the old lady of you three?

LADY BOUNTIFUL. I am.

ARCHER. God be praised! Madam, my master is in distress, and the fame of your ladyship's charity and skill have drawn me hither to implore your ladyship's help.

LADY BOUNTIFUL. Why, sir, what is the matter?

ARCHER. I fear that my unfortunate master is this minute breathing his last.

LADY BOUNTIFUL. Your master? Where is he? — Scrub!

ARCHER. At your gate, madam. Drawn hither by the appearance of your handsome house he came up the avenue to view it nearer; and he was taken ill of a sudden with a sort, I know not what, and there he lies.

LADY BOUNTIFUL. Scrub! Scrub! — Is your master used to these fits?

ARCHER. Oh, yes, madam. Frequently I have known him to be unconscious for whole nights at a time.

LADY BOUNTIFUL. Is it chilblains, think you?! Is he stiff and rigid?!

ARCHER. As a plank, madam.

LADY BOUNTIFUL. (*Happily*) Oh, I was afraid of that! I may have to remove his liver. Are his digits swollen up like hams? Do his eyes bulge, secreting a yellow pustular material?

ARCHER. Exactly so. But God's Breath, madam, he's a-dying. A minute's care or neglect may save or destroy his life.

(ENTER SCRUB.)

SCRUB. Yes, milady?

LADY BOUNTIFUL. Run into the avenue where you'll find a gentleman and bring him here, — quickly, quickly! It could be rampant *alopoetia meningus*, or my own discovery, *Peloponnesus Aquaticus* — or GREEK WATER DISEASE. Oh, come with me, I'll see him brought in myself!

(Exeunt LADY BOUNTIFUL, ARCHER and SCRUB.)

MRS. SULLEN. (*Bursts out laughing.*) Ha, ha ha, ha, ha.

DORINDA. Why, sister, how can you laugh when the poor gentleman — whoever he is — may be dying at this very moment.

MRS. SULLEN. Aye, aye — the poor gentleman! Did you not shudder to hear of those nights when he is without consciousness whatever? — Sister, I have a sort of prophetic fit, and I think I can tell you: the man will live.

(ENTER CHERRY from another door, in great anxiety with a shawl thrown over her head.)

CHERRY. Madam, good Madam, I must speak to you —

MRS. SULLEN. Why, Cherry, —

CHERRY. I cannot catch my breath — I come to warn you, — those two gentlemen from the inn — they must not see me here —

MRS. SULLEN. Dorinda, go help your mother bring the gentleman in. I'm sure they'll need you.

DORINDA. Indeed, if I could help —

(EXIT DORINDA.)

CHERRY. Madam, you are all in danger. Believe me, they are rogues and rascals — at least I think they are — oh, I don't know what to think!

LADY BOUNTIFUL. (*From offstage.*) Bring him this way.

CHERRY. They are coming now! Hide me. For I shall not go until I tell you what I know.

MRS. SULLEN. Come, hide in this china closet.

(EXIT CHERRY.)

MRS. SULLEN. I'll call you when they've gone.

(ENTER SCRUB and ARCHER carrying AIMWELL in a chair, followed by LADY BOUNTIFUL and DORINDA.)

LADY BOUNTIFUL. Look! Look! The man is unconscious! He barely breathes! Scrub, get you to my dispensary. Bring me the potion I made this morning of dried eel, grated squid beak and the mucous membrane from the cow fetus. I'll have him drink it.

(AIMWELL sits bolt upright and tries to get away.)

LADY BOUNTIFUL. Hold him down! Hold him down! His fit is very strong! Bless me, how his hands are clenched!

ARCHER. *(To DORINDA.)* You, madam, I pray you help us. Take his hand and open it, if you can, while I hold his head.

DORINDA. Poor gentleman! Oh, he has got my hand and he squeezes it unmercifully.

LADY BOUNTIFUL. 'Tis the violence of his convulsion, child. Why what's the matter with the foolish girl, I have got this hand open with the greatest of ease.

ARCHER. No doubt, he is in delirium and fancies this is the hand will save him.

LADY BOUNTIFUL. *(Manipulates AIMWELL's head and limbs in unnatural directions.)* Look! Look how his head lolls and his eyes roll backwards! Why his tendons have the consistency of calves' foot jelly. *(Happily)* It's a convulsion in a million, sir! Where did his illness take him first, pray?

ARCHER. Today at church, madam. Something entered his eye and inflamed his head and was straight conveyed to his heart.

LADY BOUNTIFUL. Poor gentleman! I shall need the forceps for this one. Scrub, turn him over and pull his trousers down. *(AIMWELL tries to get away again.)* Hold him steady!

ARCHER. Wait! His eyes are open now! He recovers! How does your lordship?

AIMWELL. Martin's voice, I think.

ARCHER. Could your lordship release this lady's hand? It is causing her pain.

DORINDA. No don't release it. Please! I would fain help him recover.

AIMWELL. God above! Is this an angel before me? Am I in Paradise?

LADY BOUNTIFUL. Delirious, poor gentleman. I fear we'll need the bone saw.

AIMWELL. No, no! I am much better. Thank you, madam. But where am I?

ARCHER. In very good hands, sir. You were taken just now with one of your old fits, — under the trees, — and her ladyship has taken you in and has miraculously brought you to yourself, as you see.

LADY BOUNTIFUL. It was nothing, sir. It's what I'm trained for.

AIMWELL. *(Rising, to DORINDA.)* Madam, if you are not in my dream...I must ask your pardon. I have hurt your hand.

DORINDA. Sir, it is...forgotten, already. *(They gaze at each other.)*

LADY BOUNTIFUL. See, his eyes glaze over. We shall need the pig intestine.

AIMWELL. No, no, madam! I am confounded with shame for your inconvenience and ask to wait upon you tomorrow with my thanks.

LADY BOUNTIFUL. Never, sir. You should not go outside yet. You must first to my dispensary where I have something that will restore you wholly. Come, Dorinda, you will learn from this.

(They all go out leaving ARCHER bowing beside the door for MRS. SULLEN to pass.)

ARCHER. Madam?
MRS. SULLEN. Pray go, sir. I shall follow presently.

(ARCHER glances at her with a smile and goes out.)

MRS. SULLEN. *(To the audience.)* Heaven help me! Is there no protection for a woman against the impertinence of a man's eyes? None! The whole house is bent on pushing me into this impudent fellow's arms, and even I, who know that he is an imposter laughing at us all for country fools, even I could not say that I despise him. Alas is not there the whole anatomy of a woman's soul? With half our heart we would turn the tables upon 'em, expose their arrogance, heap ridicule upon their complacency, and drive them in triumph from the scene; but *(Putting her hand on her heart.)* with the other half — Oh, Eve, Mother of us all! — we would have their admiration, play the fool for their flattery, and stifle our reason so that we might believe their protestations. Oh, there is a warfare in our natures that only love can put an end to, and one more humiliation from this master-footman and I shall be his servant in a bondage compared to which slavery itself is the freedom of a bird. I must haste to join them, for if he came in that door alone I'd be —

(ENTER ARCHER.)

ARCHER. Madam!

MRS. SULLEN. God help us all! Sir?

ARCHER. The graciousness of your attention, madam, emboldens me to ask you if you might consider engaging me in your service, madam?

MRS. SULLEN. Why, sir, we live in the country; our needs are few.

ARCHER. The service I offer you can only be judged by trial.

MRS. SULLEN. I fear that your service would be too costly.

ARCHER. It is true, madam, that without recompense I would like to perish, but I would ask no more than many men receive, knowing that from your ladyship's hand it would be reward richer than a miser's dream.

MRS. SULLEN. (*To the audience.*) What did I tell you? Are not these lies for which whole kingdoms have been lost? — What recommendations, sir, do you bring from your previous situations?

ARCHER. None, madam, and I deserved none, for I never gave true service before.

MRS. SULLEN. Is that an advantage?

ARCHER. Indeed it is, for I have neither been rendered dull by routine, nor do I come with the vainglory of past triumphs.

MRS. SULLEN. (*Aside to the audience with a gesture of surrender.*) If this be a footman, I am ready for the kitchen! — Would you be willing and courteous to all members of the household?

ARCHER. No, madam, unendurable. The zeal of my devotion to you would permit no one else to usurp my time.

MRS. SULLEN. Should I be obliged, however, to dismiss you, would you take it without rancor?

ARCHER. Hellfire and damnation, no! (*Kneeling*) All that I ask of you, Madam, is a lifetime's engagement. Your life and your heart and beyond that nothing.

MRS. SULLEN. Sir, I wonder that you can affect so great a passion for a woman whom you take to be a fool.

ARCHER. Madam?

MRS. SULLEN. Nay, do not rise; for since you think so

lightly of me, I could wish to see you forever in this ridiculous position. Do you think that I believe you to be a footman? And that your friend, who but now pretended imperfectly to an illness, is Lord Robert Aimwell? No, sir, you are imposters — whether from knavery or from sport, I do not know.

ARCHER. Madam, we are.

MRS. SULLEN. Confession is easy, sir, when one has been found out. I am your servant, sir.

ARCHER. Madam, if we are imposters, give me one day, one half a day, to show you that we have meant neither harm nor mockery here.

(Sounds of SULLEN roaring off stage.)

ARCHER. Your husband is coming, madam —

(ENTER SULLEN, from the hall, still more drunk.)

SULLEN. Brother Martin! Why, where y'been brother? And there's my wife. God's name you've all been hiding.

MRS. SULLEN. Sir, you are drunk, and I'll leave you.

SULLEN. Wife! This man is my brother, and so he's your brother. You shall treat him kindly and give him a kiss.

MRS. SULLEN. I promise you I have treated him kindly, as I think he'll vouch for, and now I'll take my leave.

SULLEN. (*Roaring*) Promises or no promises, I'll break every chair that's here and all the windows too, if you'll not do what ye should.

ARCHER. Brother Sullen! Be —

SULLEN. I'll pull down the house! Yes or no?

MRS. SULLEN. My love, stop shouting. Since you wish it, I shall kiss your brother for you. — Sir, your cheek. (*She kisses him on the cheek.*) So much to save a broken chair.

ARCHER. And this for the table, madam.

(*He kisses her on the lips, in earnest.*)

MRS. SULLEN. ...And this for the breakfront.

(*She kisses him with great passion.*)

SULLEN. So! What's a house without friends?

(*ENTER LADY BOUNTIFUL in a great rage followed by DORINDA, weeping, AIMWELL and SCRUB.*)

LADY BOUNTIFUL. Thieves! Robbers! I'll not have it! I'll not be so abused! Are you the master here or no?

SULLEN. Nay, mother you must meet my brother, — brother Martin —

LADY BOUNTIFUL. Sir, you are no Lord Robert Aimwell! Daughter Sullen, you know Lord Aimwell as well as I do — imposters! Rogues!

LADY BOUNTIFUL. Explanations! Lies! I'll not hear 'em. God's breath! I'm the kindest woman in Staffordshire, but I'll not endure rogues. Scrub, call the dogs.

SCRUB. Your ladyship, the dogs have taken so great a fancy to brother Martin here that they're like to follow him home from pure love.

AIMWELL. Madam, we need no dogs to make us withdraw. I merely hope that when your ladyship's anger has abated —

LADY BOUNTIFUL. Never!

AIMWELL. — we may have leave to present our apologies for a harmless jest. Your servant, madam.

(Exeunt AIMWELL and ARCHER.)

DORINDA. (*Swaying*) Air! I faint!

LADY BOUNTIFUL. What? Oh, now Dorinda's ill. No wonder. My son, support her into the dispensary. Come, Scrub.

(As they go out leaving MRS. SULLEN alone, she goes to the door of the china cabinet.)

MRS. SULLEN. Cherry! Cherry! Are you still here?

(ENTER CHERRY.)

CHERRY. Oh, Madam, 'tis good I've come, for the case is worse than you think. These men, madam, believe me, are no better than thieves and highwaymen.

MRS. SULLEN. Cherry! You have no proof of this!

CHERRY. More proof than I can tell, madam. This very night they aim to break into this house and rob you. *(MRS. SULLEN laughs.)* Believe me! Believe me! They are in league with a Mr. Gloss, who for four years has been a highwayman, too.

MRS. SULLEN. Ha! That is more like.

CHERRY. (*Bringing a large pistol out from under her apron.*) I have brought you this, madam, to protect yourself.

MRS. SULLEN. There is some mistake here, but I thank you. Now say nothing of this to anyone. I'll see no harm is done.

CHERRY. I think these London gentlemen are but new to robbery, madam, and I beg you not to shoot the taller one. Could you only frighten him out of his evil ways?

MRS. SULLEN. Rest easy, Cherry. He will receive enough corrections. And if he comes tonight, I shall use this pistol with the best discretion — as a warning only. It shall not be fired. My father taught me all there is to know of guns, and with this little latch upon it, just so, it cannot possibly go off.

(She shows CHERRY the latch and the gun goes off immediately with a loud report — and the two women clutch each other with a scream.)

MRS. SULLEN. Well if he does show up, God help him.

BLACKOUT

END OF ACT ONE

ACT II
Scene 1

(The inn, that night. ENTER ARCHER and AIMWELL.)

AIMWELL. Jack stop it! This is serious! Now they'll never let me in the house again!

ARCHER. Oh, we'll find a way. We did it once.

AIMWELL. And they found me out within minutes of my arrival!

ARCHER. Too bad. It was a good plan.

AIMWELL. It was a rotten plan. The moment I said I was Robert Aimwell, the old dragon started screaming the house down.

ARCHER. And you were doing so beautifully – *(Imitating AIMWELL.)* "Is this an angel? Am I in paradise?"

AIMWELL. Oh, stop it!

ARCHER. *(Imitating DORINDA.)* "O, Mother! Help! He has got my hand and squeezes it unmercifully!"

AIMWELL. Jack, would you stop it! That wonderful girl — how I hate deceiving her.

ARCHER. Ods my life, you're such an amorous puppy; you can't counterfeit a manly passion without feeling it.

61

AIMWELL. I am in love with Dorinda, and would move mountains for her.

ARCHER. I'm glad on't, for she fits our bill to the last degree. Fair of face, finely figured, of gentle nature, and rich enough to make the other attributes irrelevant.

AIMWELL. She is Aphrodite herself, arising from the sea.

ARCHER. If you think so, that's —

AIMWELL. She is Helen of Troy come back to life.

ARCHER. I'll take your word for it, but —

AIMWELL. The fair Hippolyta on her wedding day!

ARCHER. All right, enough! Whatever you please! Let her be Artemis, Callisto and the gorgon Medusa rolled all into one! And when you finish with the Greeks, you can start on the Romans. Anything to deliver us from sauntering away our evenings at a London club and be stinted to even look at a pack of cards because our impotent pockets can't afford us a guinea. But now is the time to prevent all this. To strike home while the iron is hot.

AIMWELL. Of course it is, if she'll ever see me again. We need a plan — a stratagem — to get us back in the graces of the old lady.

HOUNSLOW. (*From outside.*) Gloss, don't dawdle!

BAGSHOT. (*From outside.*) Stir your stumps, I say!

AIMWELL. Someone's coming. Let's continue upstairs.

HOUNSLOW. (*From outside.*) The pickings await and your feet are dragging!

BAGSHOT. (*From outside.*) He goes like a walrus!

(ARCHER and AIMWELL hide. ENTER HOUNSLOW, BAGSHOT.)

HOUNSLOW. The wind is high, m'dears, and sputters like a dying clergyman. Gloss, we have a robbery to commit so shift your ballast. (*They laugh.*)

ARCHER. This sounds promising. Gloss is the fellow who tried to recruit me. Let us hide, quickly. It may be something to our advantage.

BAGSHOT. Gloss! Mister Gloss! Ahoy there!

(BONIFACE ENTERS.)

BONIFACE. Not so loud, you pissing goats! I want no suspicions!

(GLOSS ENTERS.)

GLOSS. Well, gentlemen, 'tis a fine night for our enterprise.

HOUNSLOW. Dark as Hell.

BAGSHOT. And blows like the Devil; our landlord here has showed us the window where we must break in, and tells us the plate stands in the wainscot cupboard in the parlour.

BONIFACE. Aye, aye, Mr. Bagshot, knives and forks, and cups, and cans, and tumblers, and tankards. There's one tankard that's near as big as me — it was a present to the squire from his mother, and smells of nutmeg like an East India ship.

HOUNSLOW. Then you say we must divide at the top of the stairs?

BONIFACE. Yes, Mr. Hounslow — at one end of that gallery lies my Lady Bountiful and her daughter, Dorinda, and at the other Mrs. Sullen. As for the squire — He's safe enough — I have engaged him in drink, and he's more than half seas over already.

BONIFACE. It's getting late. You must set out at once or we'll miss our moment.

GLOSS. Hounslow, do you and Bagshot see our arms fixed, and I'll come to you presently. And if Mr. Martin doesn't show himself soon, we go without him. Now off with you and prepare!

HOUNSLOW. We will.

BAGSHOT. We will.

GLOSS. And remember the highwayman's sacred motto: stout heart, pride in your work, and steal anything within reach.

(Exeunt HOUNSLOW and BAGSHOT.)

GLOSS. Oh, my dear Bonny, this prize will be a galleon! — I warrant you we shall bring off three or four thousand pound! Ha! Then shall I to London where I'll sell off my horse and arms and retire forever from this life o' the road. There shall I preach the Judgment Day until it shake the rafters! I shall become a known quantity. Celebrated and dined upon. I shall skip from one parish to the next like a stone on water, preaching my way to the top, until — who knows? Could it be St. Paul's for me? Or Westminster Abbey? Is there glory ahead? And is it not glory that keeps us striving forward every day in this battle we call life? Hey?

BONIFACE. And what think you then, upon retirement, of my daughter Cherry for a wife? Eh?

GLOSS. Look'ee, my dear Bonny — Cherry "is the goddess I adore" as the song goes. But I'll not have her. The poor thing has begged me to marry her, but I've denied her the pleasure. — It is a maxim in the marriage trade that if a man could be arrested on the evidence of his wife, domestic tranquility goes out the window. Lady Bountiful awaits! I'll return with the goods.

(Exeunt GLOSS and BONIFACE. ARCHER and AIMWELL reappear.)

AIMWELL. Rogues!

ARCHER. Villains!

AIMWELL. Gone to rob Lady Bountiful's house! Why didn't you tell me, Jack!

ARCHER. I didn't know that's where he meant! He said, "a house."

AIMWELL. My poor darling girl, she'll be asleep.

ARCHER. And so will mine!

AIMWELL. Yours?

ARCHER. Mrs. Sullen.

AIMWELL. She's a beauty.

ARCHER. I know.

AIMWELL. But she's married.

ARCHER. Aye, there's the rub.

AIMWELL. Jack, what'll we do?!

ARCHER. Stop them, man! What else! This could be our chance to win the hearts of the ladies we adore! We need our swords! There could be danger afoot for Dorinda and Kate — their very lives could be at stake — though I'll warrant Kate can take care of herself in a pinch.

AIMWELL. Dorinda. The name inspires me. The risk tonight shall be all my own.

ARCHER. The devil it will. We have a job to do, hand in hand, fighting for the same cause, we both play Don Quixote tonight. Wait, a prayer first before we go — (*They both kneel. To AIMWELL.*) Close your eyes. 'Dear God, please help us preserve Dorinda and Kate from the evil intentions of Gloss and his men. And please see to it that neither Aimwell nor I is seriously injured in the process.

They hurry out. As they go, we hear knocking at the door and
*   BONIFACE hurries in.)*

BONIFACE. Coming, coming. A coach and six foaming horses at this time o'night! Some great man, I suppose, for he scorns to travel with other people.

(ENTER SIR CHARLES FREEMAN.)

SIR CHARLES. Sir, forgive me, but I'm in search of the house of one Squire Sullen, who lives with his mother, Lady Bountiful.

BONIFACE. Down the road, sir, half a mile.

SIR CHARLES. And is the family a-bed, think'ee?

BONIFACE. All but the squire himself, sir — he's in the back here, called to the bar, though he ain't a lawyer — drinking with Mr. Snort the Constable, Mr. Grabb the Exciseman, and little Yamadab the hunchbacked barber.

SIR CHARLES. I find my sister's letters gave me the true picture of her spouse.

BONIFACE. You are Mrs. Sullen's brother then?

SIR CHARLES. I am.

(ENTER SULLEN, very drunk.)

BONIFACE. And here's the squire.

SULLEN. The puppies left me asleep. *(Seeing SIR CHARLES.)* Sir.

SIR CHARLES. How do you do?

SULLEN. Not well at all, sir — I have three thousand pound a year, and I can't get a man to drink a cup of ale with me.

SIR CHARLES. That's very hard.

SULLEN. Aye, sir — and unless you take pity upon me, and smoke one pipe with me, I must e'en go home to my wife, and I had rather go to the Devil by half.

SIR CHARLES. But, I presume, sir, you won't see her tonight — she'll be gone to bed. You don't lie with your wife in this pickle, I presume!

SULLEN. What? not lie with my wife! Do you take me for an atheist?

SIR CHARLES. Why sir, to lie with your wife in this state would be a crime.

SULLEN. Nay, sir, the crime is the state of marriage. But my crime has born no fruit. It is *felonius interruptus.* A dry crime. *(Teary)* It has produced no offspring, sir, no little boy who I might teach to ride and shoot and drink — a little imp to dandle on my knee and ladle spirits down his little throat. But no matter, no matter; I can live without him and drink alone.

SIR CHARLES. Sir, I shall be happy to share a bottle with you — but over it we shall discuss your wife.

SULLEN. I'd rather we discussed the tinker's wife, or anybody's wife, just not my wife. She is a gorgon, sir; a tartar; a Scot. Except the Scots love their liquor I hear.

SIR CHARLES. And they love their wives, too.

SULLEN. Liquor and wives. The twin pillars of oblivion.

With one you drown yourself, and the other drowns you. —
Go, bring us a bottle.

(EXIT BONIFACE.)

SULLEN. Sir, you shall dine with me tomorrow and
meet my wife.

SIR CHARLES. I know your wife already, sir. She is my
sister.

SULLEN. God's Blood! — I can see it in the tilt of your
nose — and that jaw — like an angry beaver. How pleased
you must be to be rid of her.

SIR CHARLES. On the contrary, sir. I want her back.
And you don't want her, so why not part with her?
Unhappiness is catching. Let me take her off your hands.

SULLEN. No! Never!

SIR CHARLES. But if you hate her, sir —

SULLEN (*Roaring*) That is not the point! She is my
goods, my horse, my ox, my anything, as the poet says, and
she is *all mine!*

(CHERRY ENTERS and runs to the men.)

CHERRY. Help! Help! Please, sir! Help!

SIR CHARLES. What's the matter? You tremble, child,
you're frighted.

CHERRY. No wonder, sir. This very minute a gang of
rogues are gone to rob my Lady Bountiful's house!

SULLEN. How? My house!

CHERRY. I passed 'em on the way, and left 'em breaking in.

SIR CHARLES. Have you alarmed anyone else with the news?

CHERRY. No sir — I run straight here. O, I'm frighted, sir. My Lady Bountiful is my godmother; and I love Miss Dorinda so well —

SIR CHARLES. And is Mrs. Sullen there?

CHERRY. She is, sir. Do you know her?

SIR CHARLES. She's my sister! Will you guide me there this instant?

CHERRY. With all my heart, sir. Come!

(Exeunt SIR CHARLES and CHERRY. SULLEN stays and sways from drink.)

SULLEN. Break into my house?! Eh?! What?! I'll make minced meat o' the vomitous rogues! I'll split their gizzards till their plaguey guts fall out! I'll vivisect 'em from the neck downwards! (*He turns to the audience.*) You think I drink too much, don't you? Well you're right. But how would you feel if you were married to my wife? You see, getting married is easy enough; it's staying married that's the tricky part. What is so difficult about marriage? Everything. Do I believe in it? No. Why did I get married? Stupidity. Why do I stay married? Stubbornness. So here's my catechism on the marriage state: Men: If you try to please a woman, you are doomed to failure. You might as well put a cork in a volcano; it may quiet the monster down for a while, but the explosion is coming and you should stand aside. Women: If you're in doubt about the man who wants to marry you, say no. Don't do it. Unlike wine, men do not improve with age.

(He sways from drink and walks off.)

Scene 2

(A bedchamber in LADY BOUNTIFUL'S house, a few minutes later. It's dark outside. ENTER MRS. SULLEN and DORINDA. During the following, MRS. SULLEN takes off her gown and gets into her nightdress, behind a screen or perhaps in front of us.)

MRS. SULLEN. Well, sister. What think you now of m'lord?

DORINDA. I think he is a rogue and a villain for lying to us! — and I think him the handsomest man in four counties. What think you of his servant?

MRS. SULLEN. Servant! He's a prettier fellow, and a finer gentleman by fifty degrees than his master.

DORINDA. I cannot agree. To me, Lord whoever-he-is, is the finest specimen of manhood since Adam.

MRS. SULLEN. Despite his deception?

DORINDA. Perhaps because of it. I do not know. He's very romantic.

MRS. SULLEN. Ho, ho. How a little love and good company improves a woman.

DORINDA. Listen! — in the dispensary, while Mama was distract with medicines, my lord whispered in my ear and told me that I have more wit and beauty than any of my sex; and truly I begin to think the man is sincere.

MRS. SULLEN. You're in the right, Dorinda — pride is the life of a woman, and flattery is our daily bread. But I'll lay you a guinea, that I had finer things said to me than you had.

DORINDA. Done. What did your fellow say t'ye?

MRS. SULLEN. My fellow took the picture of Venus for mine.

DORINDA. But my lover took me for Venus herself.

MRS. SULLEN. Common cant!

DORINDA. My lover was upon his knees to me.

MRS. SULLEN. And mine upon his tiptoes to me.

DORINDA. Mine vowed to die for me.

MRS. SULLEN. Mine swore to die with me.

DORINDA. Mine spoke the softest moving things.

MRS. SULLEN. Mine had his moving things too.

DORINDA. Mine kissed my hand ten thousand times.

MRS. SULLEN. Mine has all that pleasure to come.

DORINDA. Mine offered marriage!

MRS. SULLEN. ...And I am married already. (*She turns away.*)

DORINDA. O sister, I've made you sad.

MRS. SULLEN. Your angel has been watchful for your happiness, whilst mine has slept regardless of his charge. I wish you joy, as you deserve. (*She weeps.*)

(ENTER LADY BOUNTIFUL.)

LADY BOUNTIFUL. Ladies, ladies, there you are! I have been looking for you everywhere. Now listen to me – I believe that I have winkled out why that horrible man, that rogue, that vagabond who calls himself Lord Robert Aimwell, imposed on us in such a deceitful manner. It only took a little logical thinking. The power of science. Oh, look how it has upset dear daughter Sullen.

MRS. SULLEN. I shall be all right.

LADY BOUNTIFUL. Good, good. Because I believe – no, I'm positive — that this supposed Lord Robert Aimwell has designs on you, my dear.

MRS. SULLEN. *Me?*

LADY BOUNTIFUL. Yes! Did you not hearken to how he spoke to Dorinda, saying "Angel" and "Paradise" and such like things? Hm? Well it was subterfuge! I'm sure of it! He was pretending interest in Dorinda in order to disguise his pursuit of you!

MRS. SULLEN. Madam, I fear you're mistaken.

LADY BOUNTIFUL. I tell you I don't trust the man one speck, one jot, one *gram*. He reminds me of the kind of patient who will not cooperate. You do your best for him, you offer him your finest medicines, your newest treatments, your best attention — and the next thing you know he's lying there dead on the table.

(ENTER SCRUB, agitated.)

SCRUB. Madam, madam, Miss Austen just arrived and is calling for you. She's seems very sick.

LADY BOUNTIFUL. Oh, Scrub, I just examined her this afternoon and she's as well as you or I. She simply craves attention.

SCRUB. She doesn't seem to be breathing properly...

LADY BOUNTIFUL. Oh, just give her a sip of juniper juice and tell her I'll be there in a moment.

SCRUB. Yes, madam. *(He EXITS.)*

LADY BOUNTIFUL. Now daughter Sullen, listen to me — I want you to be *very careful*. You may not believe it, but soon after this supposed Lord Aimwell left, I heard a gunshot, here in the house. That was another clue that has helped me deduce the mystery of this strange intrusion. You see, I think you have aroused the jealousy of your husband and that he was practicing with his pistol. My son may not look it, but he is a tiger when his jealousy is aroused; and it is my belief that if Lord Whoever-He-Is returns here to see you, there will be blood shed, and it won't be his.

MRS. SULLEN. I thank you for the warning, madam. You have pieced this puzzle together admirably.

LADY BOUNTIFUL. Not at all. I'm delighted to assist. It's always a matter of science, isn't it. *De*duction, *in*duction, *con*duction. The three ductions.

(SCRUB ENTERS.)

LADY BOUNTIFUL. Yes, Scrub?

SCRUB. It's Miss Austen, madam. She's dead.

LADY BOUNTIFUL. Oh nonsense.

SCRUB. After I gave her the medicine you said, she turned purple all over, started to shake, then dropped to the floor. Now she's not breathing.

LADY BOUNTIFUL. I tell you this woman will go to any lengths to get my attention. Pray excuse me. And if I were you, daughter Sullen, I'd pay special notice of my son tonight. A new nightdress, perhaps. Tousle your hair. Set out a little platter of blood pudding and head cheese. He is your husband. Come, Scrub.

(LADY BOUNTIFUL and SCRUB EXIT.)

MRS. SULLEN. Husband! She calls him husband. No.

Husband is too soft a name for him. Were I born an humble Turk where women have no soul nor property, there I must sit contented. But in England, a country whose women are its glory, must women be abused? — where women rule, must women be enslaved, nay, cheated into slavery, mocked by a promise of comfortable society into a wilderness of solitude? But, come, I expect my brother here tonight; he was abroad when my father saw me married; perhaps he'll find a way to make me easy.

DORINDA. Will you promise not to make yourself easy in the meantime with my lord's friend?

MRS. SULLEN. You mistake me, sister. It happens with us, as among the men, the greatest talkers are the greatest cowards. Though to confess the truth, I could love that fellow. And if I met him dressed as he should be, and I undressed as I should be — look'ye, sister, I can't swear I could resist the temptation.

DORINDA. Well, thoughts are free, sister, and them I allow you — so, my dear, goodnight.

(EXIT DORINDA. The chamber is warmly darkened.)

MRS. SULLEN. Thoughts free! are they so? (*She gets into bed.*) Why then suppose him here, dressed like a youthful, burning bridegroom —

(Here ARCHER steals through the window.)

MRS. SULLEN. — With tongue enchanting, eyes bewitching, knees imploring, *(Turns a little o' one side and sees ARCHER in the posture she describes.)* Ah!

ARCHER. (*Going toward her.*) Shh!
MRS. SULLEN. Stay back!

(She pulls out the pistol that CHERRY gave her and waves it, trying to aim. He dodges back and forth to avoid the front of it.)

ARCHER. Madam, please — !
MRS. SULLEN. Have my thoughts raised a spirit? What are you, sir, a man or a devil?
ARCHER. A man, a man, madam! Now put that down! —
MRS. SULLEN. Stay back I say!
ARCHER. Be careful!
MRS. SULLEN. Do you intend to be rude, sir? To woo me in the dark of night and make love to me?
ARCHER. No, madam, I want you to —
MRS. SULLEN. You *want* me, sir? How dare you! Do you think me some wanton creature that would lightly toss aside her wedding vows upon flirtation! In the name of wonder, whence came ye!
ARCHER. (*Approaching her.*) I came through the window, but only to w —
MRS. SULLEN. I may feel things, sir, a million things, in my heart and in my breast, but I cannot go beyond the bounds of natural pride and moral decency —
ARCHER. Yes, of course —
MRS. SULLEN. I am a woman without my sex! — I can love to all the tenderness of wishes, sighs and tears — but go no further —
ARCHER. (*Approaching*) Madam, if you would but listen a —

MRS. SULLEN. Stay back I say!

(BANG! The gun goes off loudly, almost killing ARCHER.)

ARCHER. AHHHHHHH!

MRS. SULLEN. Are you hurt?

ARCHER. No! No thanks to you! Now quiet down or you'll raise the house and ruin my trap!

MRS. SULLEN. Your trap! O God, so those *are* your intentions —

ARCHER. No, not that kind of t —

MRS. SULLEN. How dare you, sir! I'll wake the dead before I bear this!

ARCHER. No, you see —

MRS. SULLEN. Believe me, sir, I would go to you if I could.

ARCHER. It's not —

MRS. SULLEN. And yet you cannot build on that! For my most mortal hatred follows if you disobey what I command you now.

ARCHER. I beg a w —

MRS. SULLEN. And yet, you mustn't be entirely discouraged from —

ARCHER. *(End of his rope.)* MADAM, WOULD YOU PLEASE STOP TALKING AND LISTEN TO ME!!

(ENTER SCRUB in his breeches, and one shoe.)

SCRUB. Thieves! Thieves! Murder! Popery!

ARCHER. *(Draws and offers to stab SCRUB, not recognizing him in dark.)* Ha!

SCRUB. (*Kneeling*) O, pray, sir, spare all I have and take my wife! I mean my life.

ARCHER. Scrub?

SCRUB. O, sir, it's you!

MRS. SULLEN. The fellow looks as if he were broke out of Bedlam. What's the matter?

SCRUB. Oons, madam, a gang of rogues broke into the house with fire and sword! They'll be here this minute!

MRS. SULLEN. O dear God!

ARCHER. It's what I have been trying to tell you, madam! I'm here to protect you, not to ravish you!

MRS. SULLEN. (*Disappointed*). Oh. But now I recollect, you are one of the rogues yourself, come to rob the place.

ARCHER. I, madam?

MRS. SULLEN. Cherry overheard you talking with a Mr. Gloss at her father's inn.

ARCHER. I was getting him to talk so I could stop his villainy! *(To SCRUB.)* How are they armed, friend?

SCRUB. With sword and pistol!

ARCHER. Hush — I see a dark lantern coming through the gallery. Madam, be assured I will protect you, or lose my life.

MRS. SULLEN. Oh, sir, they can rob me of nothing that I value half so much; therefore, I entreat you to be gone.

ARCHER. No, madam. I'll work by stratagem. Scrub, the candles. *(To MRS. SULLEN.)* Have you courage enough to face 'em?

MRS. SULLEN. Yes, yes!

ARCHER. Then into the bed. Come hither, brother Scrub. This way — here.

ARCHER and SCRUB hide behind the bed. ENTER GLOSS
   with a dark lantern in one hand and apistol in t'other.)

GLOSS. Ay, ay, this is the chamber, and the lady alone.

MRS. SULLEN. Who are you, sir! What would you have! D'ye come to rob me!

GLOSS. Rob you! alack-a-day, madam, I'm only a poor man of the cloth; and so, madam, if you make a noise, I'll shoot you through the head; but don't be afraid, madam — (*Laying his lantern and pistol upon the table and searching her pockets.*) Ooons, these rings, madam — but don't be concerned — I have a profound respect for all living creatures — unless they make a noise and I have to kill 'em...

(Here ARCHER comes round and seizes the pistol, takes
   GLOSS by the collar, trips up his heels, and claps the pis-
   tol to his breast.)

ARCHER. Ha!

GLOSS. Aiee!

ARCHER. Hold, profane villain, and take the reward of thy sacrilege!

GLOSS. Zounds and damnation. My new recruit. Why it ain't honest!

ARCHER: Down! Down, I say.

GLOSS. O! Pray, sir don't kill me; I an't prepared!

ARCHER. How many are there, Scrub?!

SCRUB. Five and forty, sir!

ARCHER. Then I must kill the villain to have him out of the way!

GLOSS. Hold, hold, sir — we are but three, upon my honour!

ARCHER. Scrub, will you undertake to secure him?

SCRUB. Not I, sir; kill him, kill him!

ARCHER. Come, rogue, if you have a short prayer, say it.

GLOSS. Sir, I have no prayer at all; the government provides a chaplain to say prayers *for* us on these occasions. Ah!

MRS. SULLEN. Pray, sir, don't kill him!

GLOSS. Sir, I'll give you two hundred pound to spare my life! It's all I have in the wide world! No, make it four hundred.

ARCHER. (*With scorn.*) Do you expect to bribe me, sir? With four hundred pounds? All right, done. You shall live. Here, Scrub — (*Handing over pistol.*) keep him under guard. Can you do it?

SCRUB. Ay, sir. If he moves, I'll let him have it between the thighs. I mean the eyes. (*Shrieking without.*)

ARCHER. 'Sdeath! the rogues are at work with the other ladies. I must fly to their assistance. Will you stay here, madam, or venture yourself with me?

MRS. SULLEN. O, with you, dear sir, with you.

(*ARCHER sweeps her up in his arms and exeunt.*)

Scene 3

(*Another apartment in the same house, a moment later. ENTER HOUNSLOW dragging in LADY BOUNTIFUL, and BAGSHOT hauling in DORINDA; the rogues with swords drawn, the women screaming.*)

HOUNSLOW. Come, come, your jewels, mistress.

BAGSHOT. Your keys, old woman.

LADY BOUNTIFUL. Old? Old?! Why, I'll give you "old!"

(ENTER AIMWELL.)

AIMWELL. Turn this way, villains; I durst engage an army in such a cause!

(He engages 'em both. They fight vigorously. During the fighting, LADY BOUNTIFUL speaks to AIMWELL.)

LADY BOUNTIFUL. But you're a villain, sir! You came here this afternoon under false pretenses!

AIMWELL. I came to see your daughter.

LADY BOUNTIFUL. But she is married, sir!

AIMWELL. *(Still fighting, to DORINDA.)* You are?

DORINDA. No, not me. My sister-in-law.

AIMWELL. But I'm not in love with your sister-in-law. *(Gazing into her eyes.)* I'm in love with someone far lovelier.

DORINDA. Really?

AIMWELL. Yes.

LADY BOUNTIFUL. I wish someone would tell me what's going on around here...

(AIMWELL battles on valiantly, but is now in trouble.)

DORINDA. O, madam, had I but a sword to help this brave man!

LADY BOUNTIFUL. There's three or four hanging up

in the hall, but they won't draw! I'll go find something with
a point to it.

*(EXIT LADY BOUNTIFUL. ENTER ARCHER and MRS.
SULLEN.)*

ARCHER. Hold, hold, my lord — every man his bird,
pray.

*(They engage man to man. Fierce fighting. Momentarily,
ARCHER and AIMWELL are overcome. MRS. SULLEN
and DORINDA pick up their swords and fight the villains.)*

ARCHER. My thanks.
MRS. SULLEN. *(Fighting)* Pleasure.
AIMWELL. *(To DORINDA, a little put out.)* You're
awfully good at this.
DORINDA. I studied fencing as a child.

*(The women toss the swords to their heroes and the men fight
the villains again. Soon the rogues are overthrown and
disarmed.)*

ARCHER. Shall we kill the rogues?
AIMWELL. No, no, we'll bind them.
ARCHER. Aye. Good. *(To MRS. SULLEN.)* Here,
madam, lend me your garter.
MRS. SULLEN. *(Aside)* The Devil's in this fellow. He
fights, loves and banters, all in a breath.

(ENTER SCRUB.)

SCRUB. Is all well here?

ARCHER. Well, Scrub, have you secured your Tartar?

SCRUB. Yes, sir — I bound him hand and foot and mouth.

AIMWELL. Pray carry these gentlemen to reap the benefit of your experience.

SCRUB. Come on, come on, ye slimy cutthroats.

(Exeunt SCRUB with HOUNSLOW and BAGSHOT. The women talk in dumb show.)

ARCHER. *(Indicating DORINDA.)* Aimwell, regard. She is flushed and breathless. Press her this minute to marry you and gain our fortune. Speak some romantic nonsense or other. I have arranged for a French parson who awaits you in the drawing room.

AIMWELL. But how shall I get off without being observed? Wait. You bleed, Archer. That could be it.

ARCHER. 'Sdeath, you're right. This wound will do the business.

(LADY BOUNTIFUL bounds in with sword and pike, a Tartar.)

LADY BOUNTIFUL. And now I'll at 'em! Stand forth! Make way and drop your weapons! I am female and I am dangerous! — what? All gone?

DORINDA. The day is won and the villains are taken off.

LADY BOUNTIFUL. Already? O, alas I had no chance

at 'em. I would have done my worst, I swear it! (*Fencing*) Chya! Chya! Chya! But all is well.

ARCHER. True. And yet I must confess that I am wounded, madam.

MRS. SULLEN. How!

LADY BOUNTIFUL. Wounded?!

DORINDA. (*To AIMWELL.*) I hope, sir, *you* have received no hurt?

AIMWELL. None but what you may cure.

(During the following, AIMWELL carries off DORINDA.)

LADY BOUNTIFUL. Let me see your wound, sir. Ah! An ugly gash, upon my word. You must to bed, sir, at once. We may have to amputate. Scrub! Prepare my instruments! It is a dream come true!

(LADY BOUNTIFUL runs out. ARCHER and MRS. SULLEN are alone now.)

ARCHER. Come, madam, and obey your mother. You must take me to bed.

MRS. SULLEN. Are you still so bold, after entering through my window unbidden — ?

ARCHER. To save you in your hour of need!

MRS. SULLEN. So you say now.

ARCHER. Madam, how can you, after what is past, have the confidence to deny me? Was not this blood shed in your defence, and my life exposed for your protection? (*As if in real agony.*) Ah! This wound! — how I suffer!

MRS. SULLEN. I don't believe you.

ARCHER. (*Dropping the agony instantly.*) All right, fine. But look'ye, madam, I'm none of your romantic fools that fight giants for nothing; my valour is downright Swiss; I'm a soldier of fortune and must be paid.

MRS. SULLEN. 'Tis ungenerous in you, sir, to upbraid me with your services.

ARCHER. 'Tis ungenerous in you, madam, not to reward 'em.

MRS. SULLEN. How? At the expense of my honour?

ARCHER. Honour! Can honour consist with ingratitude? Do you think I would deny you in such a case?

(*ENTER a servant.*)

SERVANT. Madam, your brother is below at the gate, along with Miss Cherry from the inn.

MRS. SULLEN. My brother? Heavens be praised. (*To ARCHER.*) Sir, he shall thank you for your services — he has it in his power.

ARCHER. Who is your brother, madam?

MRS. SULLEN. Sir Charles Freeman. You'll excuse me, sir; I must go and receive him. (*EXIT MRS. SULLEN.*)

ARCHER. Sir Charles Freeman! 'Sdeath and Hell! — Aimwell's old acquaintance. (*To the audience.*) He'll discover Tom to the entire company! He knows that Aimwell is no lord, and that we are both in want of money. One word from him and our stratagem is up! Stratagem. Subterfuge. Prevarication. Is this the proper way to win a wife? I began this campaign beating the drum of commerce. But then my heart was captured and the bold tattoo turned lovingly to a minuet; and now it threatens to become a waltz, danced by a besotted suitor. Oh, how I hate myself for falling in love! Was there ever a more pathetic creature on this earth than a man in love? I think not. You can tell such a man at a glance: his lip hangs like a torn curtain; his eyes bulge with expectation; his nose is red from drinking too much; his fingers twitch from writing sonnets; he neglects his dress; he shuffles instead of walking; and when he thinks about the wedding night, he turns yellow and stops breathing. Have I become such a vile specimen? I think I have; but God help me, it's Kate who's done it, and so I march into Hell a willing victim of my own defeat. And yet...the wench is married! What can be done! And unless Aimwell has made good use of his time and said his "I do" to the parson, all our fair machine goes south into the sea like a shipwreck. If this were a play, we'd be nearing the climax. As it is, we can only hope for the best.

(*He hurries off.*)

Scene 4

(*The drawing room in the same house, a moment later ENTER* AIMWELL *and* DORINDA.)

DORINDA. Well, well, my lord, you have conquered; your late generous action will, I hope, plead for my easy yielding, though I must own your lordship had a friend in the fort before.

AIMWELL. But where is the parson?

(*ENTER FOIGARD, French Parson, with a book.*)

FOIGARD. Ah, bonsoir, bonsoir, I am Foigard and I am late and I am zorry. I 'ad to perform a 'ow you say, baptisme. Is normalement no problème, n'est pas? Water, plop, is feenished. But today, ze mozzer of ze leetle boy, she talk to me while I perform ze service and I forget about ze boy, and 'e is gasping for ze air, *argh! argh!*, and o la la, ze fuss zey make: "You could 'ave keeled 'im! 'E could 'ave died!" And zis is nonsense! I am Foigard! I keel no one. Except once, totalement by acceedent. A grown man. 'E came to me for sacrament. I say take off your sword, 'e say no. I pull eet, 'e pull eet back. I pull eet, 'e pull eet back. I pull too hard, I push it back, *pht!*, 'e's gone. But please, relax. No one ever dies of marry-ahj. Zey suffer, but zey do not die. Ha! Zat is Foigard's joke. Zo, you are bose preparèd?

AIMWELL. I'm ready.

DORINDA. And I.

(FOIGARD assumes pious stance and begins service.)

FOIGARD. *Bon.* We begin. Ahem. Dearly beloved —

DORINDA (*To AIMWELL.*) But first, one word. My lord — and in calling you "my lord", I do not err, I hope.

AIMWELL. Err, madam?

DORINDA. You have told me so little of yourself that I voyage forth on trust alone.

AIMWELL. And I shall tell you more anon… after we're married.

DORINDA. And not before?

AIMWELL. Well. No.

DORINDA. I see.

FOIGARD. Bon. Shall we begin?

DORINDA. In a moment. You see, my lord — if you are

my lord — I have a frightful example of a hasty marriage in my own family. Pray, consider just a little 'ere this step is taken —

AIMWELL. Consider! Do you doubt my honour or my love?

DORINDA. Neither. I do believe you equally as brave in both. But I am a woman and the law is the law. Once married, my lot is yours.

AIMWELL. My poor darling.

DORINDA. And yet, I know you would not lie to hurt me and so I will marry you this instant if you insist.

AIMWELL (*Aside*) She is an angel — and has gained my soul, and made it honest like her own. Parson, retire.

FOIGARD. Hm?

AIMWELL. Go now. Quickly.

FOIGARD. But I have just arrivèd.

AIMWELL. Well I'm sorry, but we have no need of your assistance now.

(FOIGARD sighs heavily with disgust and exits.)

AIMWELL. Madam, what I have to tell you will pain us both. I am all a lie — all counterfeit except my passion.

DORINDA. I know! but pray, sir, who *are* you?

AIMWELL. I am brother to the man whose title I usurped, but stranger to his honour and his fortune.

DORINDA. O, no.

AIMWELL. I am no lord, but a poor needy man, come with a scandalous design to prey upon your fortune. But the beauties of your mind and person have so won me from myself, that like a trusty servant, I prefer the interest of my mistress to my own. Farewell, goddess. (*He starts to leave.*)

DORINDA. Wait! Matchless honesty. Once I was proud of your wealth and title, but now am prouder that you lack it. (*Calls*) Parson, come back! Parson!

AIMWELL. Parson!

(*ENTER FOIGARD.*)

DORINDA. Marry us, sir. Please. This minute!

FOIGARD. Zo. Enfin. You change your mind, eh? And now you need Foigard? I am not zurprized. Eferey bodey need Foigard. But no one ever say before 'allo-goodbye like zat. But I am Foigard and I forgeeve. You are beautiful couple, you make beautiful cheeldren. I hope. But you never know. I married one couple, zey both looked like gods; but zere cheeldren were so ugly zat cows in ze fields would stop and look at zem. Ha ha. Hon, hon. Zo. *Bon.* We begin again. Ahem. Dearly beloved —

(*A servant ENTERS.*)

DORINDA. Wait!

(*Servant whispers to DORINDA. "What?" "Yes!" "Can it be!" "It is!".*)

DORINDA. I'll come! (*To FOIGARD.*) Your pardon, sir. You may retire. We do not need you any more.

FOIGARD. What!

DORINDA. (*To AIMWELL.*) Sir, you must excuse me — I'll wait upon you presently.

(EXIT DORINDA with Servant.)

FOIGARD. Zis is totalement fool-eesh! You cannot do zees! I am Foigard!

AIMWELL (*In despair.*) I'm sorry, but you heard what she said! Now go!

(FOIGARD stamps his foot and EXITS. As he goes, ARCHER ENTERS.)

ARCHER. Tom — shall I wish you joy? Are you happily married yet?

AIMWELL. No, not yet.

ARCHER. Oons, man, what ha' you been doing!

AIMWELL. O, Archer, my honesty, I fear, has ruined me. I have discovered my true self to the lady.

ARCHER. Discovered! and without my consent? Have I embarked my small remains in the same bottom with yours, and you dispose of all without my partnership?

AIMWELL. O, Archer, I own my fault

ARCHER. You may remember, Mr. Aimwell, that you proposed this folly. As you begun, so end it. Henceforth I'll hunt my fortune single. So farewell.

AIMWELL. Stay, my dear Archer, but a minute.

ARCHER. Stay! What — to be despised, exposed as a fortune-hunter and laughed at?

(ENTER DORINDA mighty gay.)

AIMWELL. Wait! By all my hopes, she comes, and smiling comes!

DORINDA. Come, my dear lord, I fly with impatience to your arms. Where's the parson? (*Calls*) Parson!

AIMWELL. Parson!

ARCHER. Parson!

(ENTER FOIGARD.)

FOIGARD. (*From offstage.*) Whatever you 'ave to say, I do not believe you.

AIMWELL. Come quickly, sir, and marry us.

DORINDA. Yes, please!

DORINDA. Come, Parson, do your office.

FOIGARD. No more tricks, zis time?

AIMWELL. None, I promise!

DORINDA. I swear!

ARCHER. Just do it, do it!

FOIGARD. *Bon. Enfin.* We begin again. Ahem. Dearly beloved —

DORINDA. And yet...

FOIGARD. Oh sacré bleu.

ARCHER. What is it, madam!

DORINDA. *(To ARCHER.)* Look'ye sir, one generous action deserves another. This gentleman's honour obliged him to hide nothing from me: my justice engages me to conceal nothing from him. *(To AIMWELL.)* I learned this minute, sir, that you are the person that you thought you counterfeited; you are the true Lord Viscount Aimwell — you are titled and rich; and I wish your lordship joy. And look! —

(ENTER SIR CHARLES and CHERRY.)

SIR CHARLES. My dear Lord Aimwell, are the rogues dispatched? Eh? Well done. I wish you happiness.

AIMWELL. Of what?

SIR CHARLES. Of your honour, sir. Your brother died as I was leaving London. You now possess the family title and estate — worth some twenty thousand pounds.

ARCHER. Twenty thousand!

FOIGARD. O la la!

ARCHER. This is good news.

AIMWELL. Good news for both of us, Jack. Dorinda's fortune is twenty thousand pound; as we agreed from the start, we shall divide stakes; so you take all twenty and I'll take the lady.

ARCHER. All twenty?

AIMWELL. I've got twenty o' my own now, so it leaves us even.

ARCHER. Ha! Ha! Dear Aimwell! Dearest friend! Good man. Fine man. Excellent friend. Best in the world.

(MRS. SULLEN ENTERS.)

DORINDA. At last a happy ending!

ARCHER. Happy, Miss, but not quite ended. For on my honor, I owe this lady here an explanation. May I tell you the truth, madam?

MRS. SULLEN. The truth, sir? From you? Why you might hurt yourself, it's so unfamiliar.

ARCHER. (*Dropping accent.*) The truth is, I am no servant.

MRS. SULLEN. The truth is, I never thought you were.

ARCHER. And what did you take me for?

MRS. SULLEN. Why a scoundrel, sir.

ARCHER. I am not a scoundrel, madam. My name is Jack Archer, I am a gentleman, and I come to you now with all my heart, and to offer it up to you.

MRS. SULLEN. But sir —

(ENTER LADY BOUNTIFUL and SCRUB.)

LADY BOUNTIFUL. Ah, sir, how does your wound? Let's see, let's see. But you should be in bed!

ARCHER. I have begged the lady to put me there.

MRS. SULLEN (*In distress.*) Enough, sir! Please! I am chained and muzzled! Bolted like Prometheus to a silent rock! Don't you understand?! I have a husband!

ARCHER. But dammit, madam, I'm in love with you!

SIR CHARLES. Your passion does you credit, sir. And I am happy to say, you're not the only one in this room who's in love.

(SIR CHARLES take CHERRY'S arm.)

MRS. SULLEN. Charles?

SIR CHARLES. Like others in their hour of need, we found solace in adversity. We rushed up the lane, rushed to your door, rushed up the stairs, then rushed into each other's arms.

ARCHER. *(Aside to AIMWELL.)* God's Breath, she's a fast worker.

SIR CHARLES. *(To ARCHER.)* You lost her, sir, I took her. Couples couple. 'Tis the way of the world.

LADY BOUNTIFUL. But Cherry is a servant girl! She

works at the inn! You are Sir Charles Freeman!

SIR CHARLES. The world is changing, madam, and soon it shall be upside-down.

MRS. SULLEN. For some, but not for all.

SIR CHARLES. Wait! This good company meets opportunely in favour of a design I have in behalf of my unfortunate sister — I intend to part her from her husband.

LADY BOUNTIFUL. You do?

DORINDA. But how?

SIR CHARLES. Gentlemen, will you assist me?

ARCHER. Assist you! 'Sdeath! I'd give my life!

AIMWELL. And I, sir!

SCRUB. And I!

FOIGARD. I would not go so far, but I will help.

CHERRY. Wait. Here he is.

(ENTER SULLEN, drunk. They all stare at him.)

SULLEN. What's this? Is me shirt-tail out? What are ye starin' at?!

SIR CHARLES. Sir —

SULLEN. They tell me, spouse, that you had like to have been robbed.

MRS. SULLEN. Truly, spouse, I was pretty near it, had not these two gentlemen interposed.

SULLEN. And how came these gentlemen here! Eh! Eh!

MRS. SULLEN. That's his way of returning thanks, you must know —

SIR CHARLES. I told you earlier, sir, that I want you to deliver your lady to me.

SULLEN. Humph.

ARCHER. "Humph." What do you mean by "Humph?" sir? You shall deliver her. We have saved you, and your sister, and your mother — and if you are not civil, sir, we'll unbind the rogues, join with 'em and set fire to your house!

MRS. SULLEN. Hold, gentlemen — all things here must move by consent. Let my husband and I talk the matter over and you shall judge it between us.

SULLEN. Let me know first who are to be our judges. Pray, sir, who are you, again?

SIR CHARLES. I am Sir Charles Freeman, come to take away your wife.

SULLEN. And you, good sir?

AIMWELL. Thomas Viscount Aimwell, come to take away your sister.

SULLEN. And you, pray sir?

ARCHER. Jack Archer, Esquire; come —

SULLEN. To take away my mother, I hope. Gentlemen, you are heartily welcome. Let the trial commence. And now my dear, if you please, you shall have the first word.

MRS. SULLEN. Spouse.

SULLEN. Rib.

MRS. SULLEN. How long have we been married?

SULLEN. By the almanac four years — but by my account four centuries.

MRS. SULLEN. Pray, spouse, what did you marry for?

SULLEN. To get an heir to my estate.

SIR CHARLES. And have you succeeded?

SULLEN. No!

ARCHER. The condition fails. One point to the lady. The score is one to naught.

AIMWELL. Pray, madam, what did you marry for?

MRS. SULLEN. To support the weakness of my sex by the strength of his, and to enjoy the pleasures of an agreeable society.

ARCHER. And are your expectations answered?

MRS. SULLEN. No.

SIR CHARLES. And what are the bars to your mutual contentment?

MRS. SULLEN. In the first place, I can't drink ale nor hunt with him.

SULLEN. Nor can I drink tea or dance with her!

MRS. SULLEN. I hate cock-fighting and racing!

SULLEN. And I abhor ombre and piquet!

MRS. SULLEN. Your silence is intolerable!

SULLEN. *Your prating is worse!*

FOIGARD. One point for ze husband, ze score is tied.

SULLEN. *(To MRS. SULLEN.)* You're impertinent!

MRS. SULLEN. I was ever so, since I became one flesh with you.

SULLEN. One flesh! rather two carcasses joined unnaturally together.

MRS. SULLEN. Or rather a living soul coupled to a dead body.

DORINDA. So, this is fine encouragement for me!

SULLEN. Yes, my wife shows you what you must do.

MRS. SULLEN. And my husband shows you what you must suffer.

SULLEN. 'Sdeath, why can't you be silent?!

MRS. SULLEN. 'Sdeath, why can't you talk?!

SULLEN. Do you talk to any purpose?!

MRS. SULLEN. Do you *think* to any purpose?!!

AIMWELL. Point to the lady, it's two to one.

MRS. SULLEN. Have we not been a perpetual offence to each other! — a gnawing vulture at the heart!

SULLEN. A frightful goblin to the sight!

MRS. SULLEN. A porcupine to the feeling!

SULLEN. Perpetual wormwood to the taste!

MRS. SULLEN. Is there a thing on earth we could agree in?!

SULLEN. Yes — to part.

MRS. SULLEN. North.

SULLEN. South.

MRS. SULLEN. East.

SULLEN. West.

MRS. SULLEN. A divorce then — as the law calls it?

(He considers. No one breathes.)

SULLEN. ...O all right.

ARCHER. Game, set and match!

ALL. Hooray!

SIR. CHARLES. Wait! *(To SULLEN.)* What of my sister's dowry sir? Upon divorce you must give it back or else she's penniless with no expectations.

SULLEN. Give it back?! Sir Charles, you may love your sister, but I love her money.

SIR. CHARLES. Then you won't refund?

SULLEN. Not a Stiver.

ALL. Oh, no.

ARCHER. Wait! Tell me what's the portion?

SIR CHARLES. Ten thousand pound, sir.

ARCHER. Well then I'll pay it upon receipt of my twenty. She shall have a dowry and do as she pleases. *(To MRS. SULLEN.)* But mark you, madam. My sole intention is to release you from the bondage that you find so detestable, that you may live as freely as everyone has a right to. You have no obligations and I want no thanks.

MRS. SULLEN. I may not thank you even once?

ARCHER. No, never.

MRS. SULLEN. Nor feel the slightest obligation neither?

ARCHER. Not a whit.

MRS. SULLEN. But may I fall desperately in love with you and stand by your side till the end of time?

ARCHER. … Well, if you must, you must.

(ARCHER and MRS. SULLEN embrace and kiss heartily.)

SULLEN. Scrub! Bring me a dram! My head aches!

ARCHER. *(To MRS. SULLEN.)* Madam, there's a country dance I heard in Shrewsbury the other day from a recruiting officer; your hand, and we'll lead it up.

(Here a dance.)

ARCHER. If a moral to this story must be found in this age of uncertainty, it is surely this: disguise is human, it is how we travel; but finding your true self within yourself is the only sure guide to happiness. Our couples here can attest as much:

Both happy in their several states we find,
Those parted by consent, and those conjoined.
Consent, if mutual, saves the lawyer's fee.
Consent is law enough to set you free.

END OF PLAY

Adrift in Macao

A hilarious musical comedy by
Christopher Durang
With music by
Peter Melnick

Set in 1952 in Macao, China, ADRIFT IN MACAO is a loving parody of film noir movies. Everyone that comes to Macao is waiting for something, and though none of them know exactly what that is, they hang around to find out. The characters include your film noir standards, like Laureena, the curvaceous blonde, who luckily bumps into Rick Shaw, the cynical surf and turf casino owner her first night in town. She ends up getting a job singing in his night club – perhaps for no reason other than the fact that she looks great in a slinky dress. And don't forget about Mitch, the American who has just been framed for murder by the mysterious villain McGuffin. With songs and quips, puns and farcical shenanigans, this musical parody is bound to please audiences of all ages. 4m, 3f (#03829)

The Clean House
By Sarah Ruhl
2005 Pulitzer Prize Finalist

This extraordinary new play by an exciting new voice in the American drama was runner-up for the Pulitzer Prize. The play takes place in what the author describes as "metaphysical Connecticut", mostly in the home of a married couple who are both doctors. They have hired a housekeeper named Matilde, an aspiring comedian from Brazil who's more interested in coming up with the perfect joke than in house-cleaning. Lane, the lady of the house, has an eccentric sister named Virginia who's just nuts about house-cleaning. She and Matilde become fast friends, and Virginia takes over the cleaning while Matilde works on her jokes. Trouble comes when Lane's husband Charles reveals that he has found his soul mate, or "bashert" in a cancer patient named Anna, on whom he has operated. The actors who play Charles and Anna also play Matilde's parents in a series of dream-like memories, as we learn the story about how they literally killed each other with laughter, giving new meaning to the phrase, "I almost died laughing." This theatrical and wildly funny play is a whimsical and poignant look at class, comedy and the true nature of love. 1m, 4f (#6266)

"Fresh, funny ... a memorable play, imbued with a somehow comforting philosophy: that the messes and disappointments of life are as much a part of its beauty as romantic love and chocolate ice cream, and a perfect punch line can be as sublime as the most wrenchingly lovely aria." — *NY Times*

THE BASIC CATALOGUE OF PLAYS AND MUSICALS
online at www.samuelfrench.com

GREAT NEW COMEDIES BY KEN LUDWIG!!

LEADING LADIES

In this hilarious comedy two English Shakespearean actors, Jack and Leo, find themselves so down on their luck that they are performing "Scenes from Shakespeare" on the Moose Lodge circuit in the Amish country of Pennsylvania. When they hear that an old lady in York, PA is about to die and leave her fortune to her two long lost English nephews, they resolve to pass themselves off as her beloved relatives and get the cash. The trouble is, when they get to York, they find out that the relatives aren't nephews, but nieces! 5m, 3f (#13757)

BE MY BABY

The play tells the story of an irascible Scotsman and an uptight English woman who are unexpectedly thrown together on the journey of a lifetime. John and Maude are brought together when his ward marries her niece. Then, when the young couple decides to adopt a new born baby, the older couple has to travel 6,000 miles to California to pick up the child and bring her safely home to Scotland. The problem is, John and Maude despise each other. To make matters worse, they get stranded in San Francisco for several weeks and are expected to jointly care for the helpless newborn. There they form a new partnership and learn some startling lessons about life and love. 3m, 3f (#04879)